The Circle

Solomon Petchers

Cover Art: Ferry Susanto

Feasters: The Circle

ISBN: 978-1-7374169-4-4

To my lovely wife,
The other half of my soul and the roots of my tree.
Unique is My Dove

Table of Contents

Chapter 1 1

Chapter 2 6

Chapter 3 23

Chapter 4 34

Chapter 5 48

Chapter 6 66

Chapter 7 73

Chapter 8 95

Chapter 9 109

Chapter 10 118

Chapter 11 129

Chapter 12 135

Chapter 13 143

Chapter 14 155

Chapter 15 164

Chapter 16 170

Chapter 17 189

Chapter 18 197

Chapter 19 204

Chapter 20 224

Chapter 21 239

Chapter 22 253

Chapter 23 268

Chapter 24 272

Acknowledgments 279

About the Author 281

Chapter 1

Nightmares

For days, nightmares taunt me, and I wake saturated with sweat. Normally, dreams come to me with a message, a warning about things to come, or a lesson played out like a dark fable. These are different. There's nothing helpful.

Every time I close my eyes, scenes from the last few days flash through my mind. The battle at Finway Aqueduct against a hoard of Feasters. Our animals perishing in the fire that drove us here to Sebastian Labs. Carissa's brother Case's malnourished Feaster body, locked in a cage in the dark recesses of Harold Croger's basement. Emily and I helplessly looking on as Andrew's blood drained out of his body, on the verge of death because Harold needed Vampire blood to cure Carissa's mother.

So, most of the time I lay awake piecing together how close we all came to death. Often, I sneak out of the room, not waking Emily or Andrew and avoiding Carissa, and make my way to another floor where I can spend time with my thoughts. I remember how the Feaster cells coursed their way through Harold's body, and how we honored his request to care for Carissa. I know it was the right thing to do, but I'm uncertain if it was the *smart* thing to do. Only time will tell, though this unsettles my brain further. In this world where the dead outnumber the living, we have survived, not because we were lucky, but because we've learned to be smart and limit our risks. What got us to this moment was a series of stupid mistakes which nearly ended everything for us. My mother would tell me there's a design to the world and things happen for a reason. Perhaps the reason is to teach us to cherish what we have and avoid rash decisions that lead to disaster. I must make sure I am better for Emily, Andrew, and now Carissa.

Finally, after several days, relentless exhaustion washes me into another dream. It's a few nights after the Feasters took over. A song plays in the background, so familiar, like remembering someone's face but not being able to recall their name. My Vampire family, fresh off a failed counterattack, sits in the living room tending to those who were lucky enough to have made it back. The air is a heavy blanket smothering us in fear, confusion, and sadness. The tears. My Aunt Gigi is sobbing over my cousin, Stevie, one of the bitten. I've never seen her like this before, or anyone in my family. So sad, so devastated. My father, always considered the rock of our clan, moves from family member to family member offering help – a cup of water for my aunt, wet washcloths for those injured – and tending to wounds. He'd worked as an orderly at the hospital for more than twenty years. With all those years of experience, he'd learned how to care for patients and offer comfort.

There's something else. Something so strange and yet oddly familiar. I can't shake the feeling that my mother is here, which I know is impossible because she passed away two years before the Feasters rose from the dead. Although my heart aches at her memory, I'm thankful she didn't have to live through any of this. Her passing devastated my father. To make matters worse, he worked at the hospital the night they brought her in. Some idiot blew through a red light and collided with her car, flipping it into a ditch. She died in my father's arms afterwards. Still, my heart tells me she's here somewhere in this place.

I scan the room, hoping to catch a glimpse of her, but I don't see her. A faint tapping echoes in the room. At first, I think it's part of the song, but its beat doesn't match. No one else notices. Time slows, and everything becomes hazy. I can't pinpoint where the tapping is coming from, so I get up to search for it. With care, I tiptoe around the living room, searching and watching the horrific scene of my family's suffering unfold. No one notices me, except for when I catch my father staring. He shoots a wink, and I return a half-hearted smile as the tapping intensifies like rain on a roof. The music becomes clearer as the reggae beats become more defined. I recall my mother's love for this style of music, which convinces me she's here even more. Without warning, the tapping turns into desperate thumps upon the front window. My hands shake as I slowly part the heavy burgundy curtains, revealing the source. I'm horrified as I'm met with my mother's blood-streaked, frantic face. She pounds the window in a frenzy, rattling the glass to the verge of shattering. Her muffled screams offer a warning which I don't understand.

"Kieran! He's not dead! He's not dead!"

"What are you saying?!" I shout back, confused.

"He's not dead!" The window shakes as she points behind me.

"Who?"

It's then, in the window's reflection, I watch Stevie's arms creep around Aunt Gigi's neck. I spin around to warn her, but it's too late. Aunt Gigi screams. My father turns to me, yelling, "Kieran! Get Emily and go upstairs!"

I'm shaken awake by my mother's warning, echoing in my head as if she's right here in the room with us. *He's not dead!* I listen for the music, but only my mother's voice rings in my ears. *He's not dead!* Although I always think about my mother, I hardly ever dream about her. This freaks me out and I breathe deeply to slow my pounding heart.

I wish I had had that warning on the dreadful night the Feasters destroyed our family, but of course, this was just a dream. I don't dream of it often, but it is never far from my thoughts, like a nightmare haunting my subconscious beneath the surface. The shouts of urgency from my father. My Aunt Rosemary's last instructions before leaving Emily and me to sacrifice herself to the Feasters. Screaming, slashing, and the breaking of bones often seeps into my thoughts whether I am dreaming or not. And then there are the images, etched into my memories like permanent wounds stitched, ripped open, and stitched again. The bloody remains, disjointed body parts, and blood of my family members was more than anyone should bear, especially for someone as young as Emily and me. Often in the moments before I fall into a deep sleep, I'm jolted awake – like the feeling of falling or racing down on a roller coaster at breakneck speed. But there's no fun in this amusement park.

There's only one regret I have from that night. When Emily and I crept out of the house, I remember seeing my father's work boots and lower body in the dark doorway of one room. I wanted to check on him. I *should* have gone to check on him. But... fear held me back. Fear of the Feasters. Fear of dying. Most of all, I feared what he'd become. Looking back, I don't think I could have handled it if the Feasters had bit him, and he had turned into one of them or if he had died. A week later, Emily and I mustered up enough bravery to go back to her house. The first place I looked was to the doorway where I had seen him last. To my surprise, he wasn't there. My guess is he must have turned. It's a shame – turning into a Feaster wasn't a fitting ending for a man who gave so much of himself to others. So, every night when I looked out of the window of the house where we lived, I searched for life, but I searched for him too, hoping to see him walking with the other Feasters so I would know what happened to him. Of course, I never did.

Chapter 2

Three Days Later

"Starsky?!" Andrew bounds over to us. I've noticed his limp is a little more prominent than it's been in the past, but his spirit is unshaken. Fun-loving and exciting to be around. Dropping to his knees, he throws his arms around Starsky, and the dog, with a slight limp of his own, showers his face with kisses and whimpers. "I've missed you, boy!" Then he turns his attention to us. "Hutch? Ms. Pickles? The goat?" The looks on our faces deliver the bad news. He reflects a second, then looks over to Starsky. He notices his singed fur and burned skin and with caution, scratches his ears, "I bet you did all you could do to help them, didn't you boy?"

Earlier that evening, Emily and I had decided we would head back to the house to see what we could salvage. I needed to satisfy my curiosity, but more importantly, check in with Emily. Something about her has been a little different the last few days. I can't put my finger on it, but her comments are short, and she doesn't stick around to talk, especially when Carissa's there. Who could blame her? We've been through a lot physically and mentally, and I'm not sure if she's had the time to process everything. Carissa has tried her best to fit in without being overbearing. Even though she doesn't know Emily the way we do, she's kept her distance as if sensing something as well. Knowing Emily, she just needs time and space. So, when I suggested going back to the house, she jumped at the opportunity.

Sneaking our way out of Sebastian Labs, we headed to the Camaro. We didn't encounter any Feasters. But as usual, we could hear them calling out in the distance. I really wanted to drive, but I didn't dare ask Emily. I remember taking drives with my father. We'd drive for hours, many times in complete silence. "Dad, are you mad at me?" I'd ask, uneasy and uncomfortable with the silence.

He'd look over at me and say, "No, buddy. I'm just clearing my head. Driving helps me." So, we would drive with no particular destination in mind. Sometimes we'd end up at the beach. Other times, we'd end up at the mall. Or we'd just circle the neighborhood a few times.

To be honest, Emily's driving makes me nervous, but she's gotten us where we've needed to go so far. I rested my thoughts on that. And besides, she's at least better than me because I have zero experience. Perhaps the drive will help her clear her mind and organize her thoughts. Knowing she gets antsy, getting out could help. It had in the past.

As we moved away from Centre Square, I decided it was a good time to approach. "So, Em? How are you doing?" She didn't break her stare from the road. I tried again using an accent our grandmother had. "Emily Estrie, how are you doing?"

She cracked a smile. "No one's called me by my last name in forever," she chuckled. "The only time that happened was when I was in trouble."

"And, if I remember correctly, you were in trouble a lot."

This made Emily crack up. She looked at me, laughing. It was good to see her smile. "You know, you were in on most of it."

"Ha! Again, I think I covered for you… a lot."

"Well, there's that too," she laughed.

"Trash can!" I shouted, pointing ahead.

"What?!"

"Trash can! Emily, look out!" I shouted. Emily's eyes fixed on the road again, she swerved and side swiped it. I put my hand on my head, "Man, you are horrible at this!" I laughed, checking my heart rate on my neck with two fingers.

"Oopsies." She blew a tuft of her red hair from her face.

I gazed at her and rolled my eyes. "So, seriously. How are you?"

"You keep asking that. I'm not sure what you mean."

"You seem so quiet. I get if you're standoffish with Carissa, but with Andrew and me? You've never been like this."

She was silent and appeared to mull over her thoughts. Finally, she said, "I'm sorry. It's just hard to process all of this. I mean, a few days ago, we were so close to losing Andrew. We've lost everything else. Now, we're living at Sebastian Labs and trusting this girl who's still connected to Harold and the cure. Something doesn't feel right." I had had a feeling this was on her mind. I waited for her to finish. "Now, I've been having these dreams the last few nights."

"Dreams? I thought that was my department."

She flashed a quick smile. "Dreams of the fight in the hallway at Sebastian Labs. I see Feasters on top of you. And — and I'm trying to clear my mind and get to a place where I can help you." Tears formed in the corners of her eyes. "But I can't. I can't help you. I watch as Feaster after Feaster take bites out of you. And then, the unthinkable happens." Her voice faded. "By the time I'm able to go full Vampire, you change into one of them. You come after me and I raise my bow."

"Do you do it?"

"No, I can't. Every time you get close, I wake up."

"Man, that's heavy. I can see why you haven't been yourself," I said.

"You think? It's all that's on my mind. So, every time I'm around any of you, I feel either sad or mad or..." Tears trickled down her cheeks. "It's so hard to process. So, it's just better to be alone with my thoughts."

"Em, I totally get it. But you do know that we're here for you. Whatever you need, we'll help."

"I know. It's just hard to ask for anything with *her* around."

"Carissa?" I asked, even though the answer is obvious.

"Yeah. She's part of the reason everything is the way it is."

"Just because she's related to Harold, doesn't make her guilty. Her association has nothing to do with the horrible things Sebastian Labs has done. She's just a teenager. Like you, and Andrew, and… and me."

"I want to believe that, but I'm having a hard time separating the two." Her tone shifted to frustration. "Look, I know we made a deal with Harold. I mean, seriously, he had the nerve to call us monsters when he was the monster all along. What he did was far worse than anything our kind would ever do. He ended the world as we know it. And just because he gets bitten. Just because he's defeated, he pleads with us to save Carissa. What if Marisol hadn't bitten him? What then, Kieran?"

These same thoughts had crossed my mind as well. "Well, things would be very different."

"I know. Andrew would be dead. We may have been murdered or have become murderers." Emily's fingers tapped aggressively against her temple. "These thoughts run through my mind like a labyrinth with no way out. So yes, something's wrong."

As we turned onto our street, the destruction of our house came into focus. Slamming on the brakes, Emily stopped the Camaro several feet from the curb. The front no longer existed. From outside, through the smoldering haze, we could see into the living room through to the kitchen; every wall was charred black and still smoking.

If it wasn't for a day of rain, the house wouldn't be standing. This place which once served as our place of safety now sat an empty shell. I turned to look at Emily, and her face told me she needed more time accepting Carissa as a member of our group.

We stepped out of the Camaro and searched for Feasters. The zombies that had ignited on the lawn as we escaped lay grouped together in a molten heap like discarded, charred marshmallows at a campfire. Protruding out of the mound, fingers and legs moved, eyes blinked, and jaws opened and closed, incapable of freeing themselves. Moving closer, we could hear their muffled groans which intensified at the prospect of food. *What mindless machines they are!* I thought.

Without breaking our horrified stares, we moved past them. There wasn't another Feaster in sight as we ascended the two-step concrete stoop – the only thing that looked familiar – and we crossed the threshold of the doorway and into the house. The acrid smell of smoke and death filled our senses, burning our eyes. Without making a sound, we moved to the doorway leading to the basement. The first thing we noticed on the charred door was the hole at the bottom. "How did that get there?" Emily asked.

Looking in, we got our answer. Hutch laid lifeless. The flames spared his body, but the smoke proved too much. Tears cooled my warm cheeks as Emily leaned against me. "Oh Hutch, you were such a good boy." We stood in silence thinking of all the fun our animals brought into our lives. "Should we check where the others are?"

Without replying, I descended the stairs where our worst fears were realized. The goat and Ms. Pickles laid lifeless, side by side.

BAM! Startled, I looked up at Emily. She had slammed her fist through the wooden two by four in the wall frame. "This is exactly what I'm talking about!"

"What?"

"This is exactly the reason accepting Carissa is going to be so difficult. Everything is the way it is because of that family! We've lost everything!" She pointed out into nothingness.

"We have each other."

Emily rolled her eyes. "Yeah, well, we lost everything else." Emily made a sweeping motion with her hands. "I mean, c'mon Kieran, look at this place!"

I nodded and couldn't offer a counterargument. I was as frustrated as she was. I looked back one more time at what was left of the basement and our animals. "Where's Starsky?" We panned the room one more time looking for him. "The hole?"

"What do you mean?"

"What if Starsky made that hole in the door? You know how he's always banging on it with those enormous paws whenever we're gone too long? Maybe he escaped."

Emily mulled that over. "He probably didn't get too far. Flames engulfed this place. Even if he did, I don't think he could have survived."

"Well, here's to hoping." When we got to the top of the stairs, I noticed the fire had ravaged a hole through the roof of the house. Through the haze of smoldering wood, the moon shone through like a beacon, illuminating what remained of the room. It didn't look like there was much left of the upstairs, but I recalled that upon pulling up to the house, the garage remained intact. The melted hinge left the door leading to the garage askew. The common wall shared with the house still smoked, but most of the garage stood unscathed. As we gathered what we could find – some clothing and gear we could use on runs, boots, and Emily's crossbow – a whimper alerted us that we weren't alone. On the floor by the rolling garage door, damaged when Emily *oopsied* the Camaro into it on our way to rescue Andrew, rested Starsky. Patches of his fur singed, and he lay motionless. His nose peeked out of the unhinged garage door.

We rushed to his side and comforted him, assessing his injuries. His tail wagged with the strength he could muster, but the rest of him remained still. He struggled for each breath. I figured he wouldn't have survived if he hadn't found the broken door leading outside exposing him to fresh air. "I guess we were right about how the hole in the basement door got there," I said, pointing to his front paws: splintered, swollen, and bloodied.

"Aww, Starsky. You tried to save them, didn't you?" Emily said.

I moved to the cabinet where we'd stored some medical supplies and set out to remove splinters and clean Starsky's wounds.

He showed little resistance. We finished by wrapping gauze around his paws. Emily poured some water into a bowl and much to our surprise and with some encouragement, Starsky drank. After we gathered what we could, I carried him with the care of a newborn baby to the Camaro and rested him in the backseat. Emily and I stared at the charred remains of a place we once called home. The three of us had shared many stories, laughs, and tears within its walls. It was hard to believe we would never return there to live.

Emily shifted the car into gear and started back to Sebastian Labs. When I looked back to check on Starsky, I saw it. It was such an unusual thing to see that I questioned it, but when I saw it again, it convinced me. Headlights. As we passed Washington and moved toward Adams, I saw them as they crossed the intersection along Washington. A few blocks later, as we crossed Monroe, I noticed them again, this time more clearly as they slithered like a snake across the intersection. The feeling of seeing headlights felt so peculiar and out of place in this post-apocalyptic world. Aside from us, I couldn't recall the last time I had even seen a car driving on the road. There were plenty of cars left over: some parked neatly and unused since the outbreak, others frozen in the middle of streets or onto sidewalks or into other cars and even trees. Each with a tale to tell, but to see them driving on the road was a different story.

"Hey, did you see that?" I asked, wondering if Emily did.

"Yes." Of course she had. Very little got past her.

Silence filled the space before a bit of frustration settled in. "Is that all you have to say?"

Breathing with even breaths, she responded, "I was thinking about the last time we saw lights."

I released an uncomfortable chuckle as I thought back to the last time. "Yeah, that didn't turn out too well, did it? It's bizarre." Wasn't that the truth? That last time almost ended up being the last time for anything and everything. "We don't see anyone but some fresh faces trolling with the Feasters for a year and a half, and now, the living are everywhere. What's going on?"

"I don't know. I'm thinking the same thing," Emily said. It's scary how much we're alike.

"So, what are we going to do about it?"

"The lights? What do you think?" Emily cocked her eyebrow.

"Well," I started, "It could be nothing or…"

"Or?"

"Or, it could be something. My fear is, what if it *is* something and they're following us? The last thing we want to do is to lead them back to Sebastian Labs."

"True. So?" Emily asks, coaxing me.

"So, it sounds like we need to go chasing pretty lights again," I said with hesitant conviction.

"I thought you might say that," Emily said as a smile curled at the corners of her lips. "You're gonna want to hold on." Emily slapped the switch to turn the lights off and throttled the Camaro through the streets, whipping past Jackson and Van Buren, weaving around cars, trash cans, and Feasters. Upon reaching Harrison Street, she shouted, "Here we go!" She stepped on the brakes and cut the wheel hard to the right. The Camaro pitched. Once it straightened, she fed it gas, which caused the tires to squeal as she held the wheel hard to the right. We spun until we faced the opposite direction. She jammed on the brakes, and we came to a jolting stop. I looked around, panicked, and found the Camaro parked with the precision of an experienced stunt driver next to the curb.

I felt my face grow flushed before realizing I was holding my breath, so I exhaled sharply, "Well, that wasn't very subtle."

I glanced at Emily. Her huge smile was only matched by her wild red hair stuck up at all ends. "I always dreamed of doing that. Not bad for the first time. Yes!" Her gloved fist slammed against the ceiling of the Camaro.

Shaking my head, still recovering, I said, "Next time, you can give a head's up." I glanced back at Starsky, and it appeared he hadn't even noticed the commotion.

"I would've, but I didn't even know it was gonna happen. I just… reacted."

"So, now what?"

"We wait." Emily shifted back to her usual serious demeanor.

"I'd feel better if we waited outside of the car. In the shadows. Just in case they *are* following us and spot the car and we have to fight." Emily nodded in agreement. Her wild parking job attracted some Feasters. I pulled out my machete and drove it into the skulls of two of them. Emily made quick work of one of them at short range with one swift movement and then armed her bow, dropping another one approaching on my side of the Camaro. We dragged the Feasters out of the street, and she retrieved her arrow.

Together we crouched in the shadows and waited. "While we're waiting, can we go back to our conversation about Carissa and Sebastian Labs?" I asked her.

"What about it?"

"I don't think you need to force yourself into accepting Carissa. I mean, I get it. It's a lot to take in. Take your time. Here's what I think. I know it's only been a few days, but even you have to admit, Carissa's trying. And... and I know you are too. Just give her some time to find her place. Just play nice." I chuckled. It's a phrase our parents used with us when Emily and I would get on each other's nerves or get too competitive.

Emily placed her gloved hand into mine and gave it a gentle squeeze. She nodded her head.

Just then, we spotted headlights coming along Harrison towards us. They reached the intersection, and an older black van came to a stop. The kind you see in movies where special government agents race up to a suspect and throw him into it. We waited about thirty seconds, but it felt like forever. Glancing at Emily, it looked like she was holding her breath, her eyes glaring. The brake lights went dark as the van shifted into gear and drove off at a slow speed, as if it was still looking for us.

"Well, there's no doubt in my mind. They were following us," Emily said.

"Yeah, but why?"

She shook her head, "Maybe they're like us and are just surprised to see someone else who's, well, not dead."

"We're going to follow them, aren't we?" I asked, knowing the answer.

"You know me so well," she smirked, blowing a tuft of hair out of her eyes. We hustled back to the Camaro. "Let's see how this feels," Emily whispered, determination glinting in her eyes. Emily brought the car to life and set it into drive. With the lights off, we followed for several blocks and out of the neighborhood. Moving at a slower pace than I'm sure Emily wanted, she maintained a comfortable distance. Nothing told us we were noticed, and after several turns which made me think they were still looking for us, it slowed near a gated industrial area on the outskirts of town where there were offices, businesses and a warehouse. The passenger side door opened, and a figure dressed in dark clothes stepped out and rolled the gate open. The van drove through. As they crossed the gated threshold, the figure, a woman with her hair pulled back tightly in a ponytail, caught sight of a Feaster. With the poise of a lion tamer, she walked up to it and dropped him with some sort of blade. She stood over the body, examining it while she wiped her weapon with a handkerchief she retrieved from her coat pocket.

As she turned to go through the gate, she stopped as if she sensed something. She turned and looked out to the street, towards us.

From the safety of some bushes we had concealed ourselves within, I looked at Emily, and as expected, she had an arrow fixed on her bow. Panning the street, the woman shrugged her shoulders and turned back around, walking through the gate. "I don't think you're going to need that," I whispered.

Emily unarmed her bow and returned the arrow to the quiver on her back. "What do you think that's all about?"

"Beats me. Are you getting any feelings about this? You know. Tingles? Emily appeared to give her body a mental check. "No. But, my heart hasn't stopped pounding."

"Yeah, I totally get it. I'd feel better if we got out of here."

"Or we could get a closer look?" Emily said to me, begging with her eyes.

"Are you kidding me?"

"I'm not saying we need to go inside, but how about a lap around the outside of the fence? C'mon, don't tell me you aren't in the least bit curious. Like you said the last time we chased lights, if they've survived this long, then they may have resources."

"I love when you use my words against me. Besides, a lot of good that did us," I said, rolling my eyes.

"Let's just have a look around."

"Fine. But promise me we won't do any more than that," I pleaded.

"Cross my heart," she replied and pouted her bottom lip. She turned and led the way along the shadows.

Lined with trees and low-lying brush, the warehouse sat in darkness. The bushes offered a good place to camouflage. We moved around along the fence, branches reached out and scratched at our clothes as we moved to the back of the building. Out of one window, a pale light flickered. Two silhouetted figures appeared to be engaged in a heated conversation. One figure towered over the other, pointing like a father scolding a child. The other one leaned in, offering a counterargument. Then, in the next instant, the larger figure shoved the other one. The smaller person threw their hands in the air in frustration and walked away. The larger one moved to the window, gazing into the night. I tried hard to see his features, but only darkness outlined his face.

Emily and I shot looks at each other. Emily must have felt the tingles as her hand rubbed the back of her neck.

"Can we get out of here? I don't like this one bit," I begged.

Emily paused a moment before nodding her head and pointing in the direction we had come. Back at the Camaro, the car sat idly. We looked over the warehouse, trying to make sense of what we had seen. I looked back to check on Starsky, and then turned to Emily whose face, etched in thought, stared straight ahead. "Hey, are you okay?"

Silence sat between us for a moment before she answered, "That was weird, right? I mean, first we're followed. Then, this building. I've never ventured out this far before. How many of them do you think there are?"

"Well, at least three for sure."

"Why such a big place for just three people?"

I hadn't thought about that. "Good question."

She paused, collecting her thoughts. Then she whispered in reserved amazement, "She was so calm when she took out that Feaster. Went right up to it and didn't even flinch. Weird, right?"

"Well, what about the window?" I knew she hadn't forgotten but I wanted to know her thoughts.

"What do you think they were arguing about?"

"I wish I knew," I wondered. "If they were following us, do you think their argument was because we lost them?"

"That would make sense *if* they were following us."

"You said you thought they were," I reminded her.

"I know. I'm just hoping that we're blowing this out of proportion. The last few days may have made me even more skeptical," Emily sighed as she finished. Knowing her the way I do, I knew she was just trying to convince herself.

"Let's head back to Sebastian Labs. I'm sure Andrew's getting worried."

Emily threw the Camaro into gear and with caution, reversed down the block just in case anyone inside the warehouse was looking outside. After we were a decent distance away, Emily spun the Camaro around and drove back to Sebastian Labs.

By the time we got inside, Starsky had a little more energy and walked down the hallway as if sensing something. Limping along, he sniffed the air and picked up his pace. As he rounded the corner, we heard Andrew's voice. "Starsky!"

Chapter 3

Another Project

"He sure did. When we got to the house, we noticed a pretty big hole torn in the bottom of the basement door. Looks like Starsky clawed through the door to free Hutch, Ms. Pickles, and the goat, but they didn't make it," I tell Andrew.

As Andrew checks over Starsky's injuries, he asks, "Where'd you find him?

"In the garage," Emily spits, frustration in her voice. "Halfway to dead. We didn't even notice him in the mess, but he called out to us. He couldn't move very well and didn't even put up a fuss when we pulled the splinters out of his paws."

Then we hear Carissa's footsteps from the hallway. She turns the corner, all dressed up, but upon seeing us caring over Starsky, she stops in her tracks. Unsure of what to say, she stammers, "Is – Is that one of your dogs?" When she gets a little closer and sees the awful shape he's in, her eyes pool with tears. "Oh my goodness, I'm so sorry. Were you able to find the others?"

Emily cocks an eyebrow, never one to miss a dig however subtle it may be, and points out, "Well, the others didn't have a chance." Her stare locks into Carissa's eyes.

"Again," the tears in Carissa's eyes spill down her face, "I'm so sorry." She turns and runs down the hallway, her cries echoing.

Emily squats down next to us. "See, that's what I'm talking about. We can't trust her when things get tough. She's not a fighter. In an instant, once the odds become too tough, she will turn and run. We are going to spend the rest of our lives having to protect her. She's a delicate flower. It's the stinking apocalypse, and she's all dolled up like she's ready for a trip to the mall."

"C'mon, Em. She's really trying," Andrew states.

"I'm not saying she's not trying. I'm saying that caring for her is going to be like caring for a baby. She's defenseless," Emily spits in exasperated whispers.

"Well, we know it's going to take time. And, you know, that's literally all we have. We have enough supplies for a month or two at least," I say.

"Yeah, so. Say what you need to say, Kieran."

"Well, since we have all this time and you think Carissa is such a liability, why don't you take some time to train her into a warrior?"

"A warrior? Carissa? HA! She is not warrior material," Emily laughs, mocking the idea.

"Well, how about something less princessy? She can be your little pet project," Andrew suggests.

Emily scoffs at this. "I don't need a project." She goes quiet, but I know her well enough to know she doesn't hate this idea, and her sudden silence is the proof.

"Emily, out of the three of us, you're the one to do it. Look what you did with your last project," I say, trying to convince her.

"Last project?" Emily and Andrew say in unison.

"Yeah," I cock my head towards Andrew in quick nods. "You know," I say with a big smile across my face, until Andrew realizes I'm digging at him.

"Hey! What the heck? I wasn't anyone's project," Andrew laughs, amused and insulted at the same time.

"He's not wrong," Emily laughs out loud. It's good to see her acting like herself, even if it is just for a moment. "You couldn't even swing that bat from both sides. You had one move, lefty. And everything had to be with full force. You would tire yourself out after just three swings. Also, you didn't know how to use your environment to help you. Now, look at you. Remember what you did in front of Carissa's house with the minivan? I take full credit for that." She finishes. By the time she's done, Andrew and I are smiling at her. She takes notice. "What?"

"You know what," I say back to her.

"Fine," she announces, standing up and stomping her feet. "I don't want to hear I'm too tough on her." She walks down the hallway towards our room.

"I wasn't that big of a project," Andrew calls after her.

"Yes, you were," Emily's voice sings as she walks further down the hall.

Andrew turns to me, "Was I?"

"It doesn't matter, buddy. Look at you now. You're a warrior. How you got there doesn't matter." I turn my attention to Starsky's wounds on his paws.

"Well," Andrew admits, "I guess I needed a *little* help."

"That's the spirit. Don't feel insulted. I've learned a lot from Emily, too." Andrew nods, satisfied with my answer. "I just didn't learn as much as you've had to."

Andrew sits up straight as if clocked with something. "You're a jerk," he laughs.

"I know." I shoot him a wink.

"But seriously, Emily's having a hard time accepting Carissa after all that's gone down. Going back to the house didn't help either. When we found Hutch, Ms. Pickles, and the goat, I thought she was going to break through the remaining beams of the house."

"I understand. I catch my mind racing with wild thoughts too. At any point, any of us or all of us could have died." I nod. "But Carissa's trying. She is."

"That's what I told her. Just keep an eye on Emily. Talk her off the ledge, if needed. This won't be easy. We need to be thankful for what we have right now and not focus on what we've lost." Andrew nods his head in agreement.

As if on cue, we hear Carissa returning to us. The clickity-clack of her fancy shoes gives her away. "She's going to be an enormous project," Andrew whispers to me out of the side of his mouth. I cover my face with my hand, hiding my amusement.

"I brought some supplies that may help with your pooch," Carissa murmurs, her arms full with some medical supplies.

"Starsky," I say.

"Excuse me?"

I smile and tell her, "Our pooch. His name is Starsky."

"Oh, so cute! Reminds me of an old show my parents used to watch."

I sit up straight with a smile, "That's how we named him. Our parents loved that show too."

"Hmm. It's funny how we hold on to the little things we treasure," she chuckles. Then she sets to checking on Starsky's injuries. With the care of a nurse, she removes the gauze we hastily put on his splintered paws. Andrew rests Starsky's head on his lap while Carissa plucks the remaining shards of wood. Aside from a few whimpers, he offers little resistance. After Carissa pulls all she can, she lathers his paws with some ointment. Finally, she rewraps the paw with fresh gauze. She repeats the same procedure with his other three legs.

"Wow, you're good at that. Where'd you learn how to do it all?" Andrew asks.

Without looking up, Carissa confesses, "My mother. She was a nurse. When this whole zombie thing happened, many people panicked. With panic comes injuries. As my father put in time here at Sebastian Labs, we set to checking on neighbors. I learned from her. I don't have a lot of experience, but I did what I could." She moves to tend the burns on Starsky by cleaning them and adding more ointment.

"I think your mother would be proud of you," I say to her.

She looks up with a half-smile through her dark brown hair, "I don't think she'd be very proud of some choices I've made. I still have a lot to make up for."

"Don't beat yourself up too much," Andrew tells her. "We've all done some things we aren't very proud of."

She purses her lips and puts the last touches on Starsky's dressing. "There we go. It's getting late for you guys. I'm sure you need to head to bed. I'll keep vigil while you sleep."

Together, we walk down the hallway. Starsky limps close to Andrew's side. We stop at the containment room that has the pigs. "We're just gonna grab a bite to eat before turning in."

"Of course," Carissa says. "Oh, I almost forgot." In the pile of supplies she had brought is a container which she hands over to me. "I microwaved some powdered eggs for Starsky. We used to have a dog. She always loved eggs. This should help with his recovery. And, if he picks at the gauze, try your best to discourage him. I will look at it tomorrow and reapply the ointment."

"Thank you, Carissa," Andrew responds, nodding his head. She places a hand behind Starsky's ear and gives him a scratch which makes him nudge into her, showing his appreciation.

She half-smiles again. "Have a good day's sleep," Carissa smiles, turns, and walks down the hallway.

As we take turns clamping down on the pigs' veins, I decide to fill him in about what Emily and I saw on our run back to the house. I start processing our encounter. The idea of seeing anyone on the roads or out in plain view has been such a foreign thing for at least a year now. But, in the course of a few days, we've seen several of the living. I've always hoped this day would come, but given all that's happened, I have to admit, I'm a little disappointed. I always pictured when we found others who had survived this long in a world where the dead out-populate the living, there would be a level of appreciation and bonding. I still hope, but part of me wonders if there's any good in what's left of this world. And, if so, how *much* is left? It feels like all we've salvaged sits in disarray. But for now, I'm thankful we have each other, a place to stay, and nourishment.

"So, Emily and I had something interesting happen to us when we went back to the house."

"I feel so horrible about Hutch and Ms. Pickles and the goat. Did it look like they suffered?" Andrew asks.

"I don't think so. Their bodies didn't burn or anything. Though inhaling all that smoke can't be much better," I say.

"We should go back and give them a proper burial," he suggests, scratching the head of Big Bertha, the largest of the pigs.

It's then I realize that Starsky, always the more curious of our pets, is resting in the corner, too exhausted to not want to check out our new friends. "Yeah, they deserve a proper goodbye." Silence envelopes us in a moment of contemplation.

"So, what did you guys see out there?"

"It was weird –," I start.

"What was? Emily's driving? You are a brave soul to get in the car with her." We both laugh.

"Seriously, we saw headlights. Like from a car. A van, actually. It kept driving across the intersections as we passed them. Like they were following us."

"Really?! That *is* weird. What do you think they wanted? Did they follow you back here?"

"No," I say. "Emily pulled off an epic move, and I'm convinced it involved luck, which turned the tables on them so we could see if they were following us."

"Let me guess. Emily thought you guys should follow them," Andrew chuckles.

"Yup."

"That's our Emily." Andrew claps in a mock applause.

"Sure is. We followed them to these buildings just on the outskirts of town." I tell him the rest about the woman getting out of the car, taking care of the approaching Feaster, and the argument we saw from the window.

"So, do you think they were following you?"

"I can't tell for sure, but my gut tells me they were."

Andrew thinks for a second before asking, "What do you think they wanted?"

"Something. Nothing. I don't know. I'm hoping they were just curious like we are. Hoping there's more than just Feasters out there."

"Here's to hoping," Andrew chuckles.

"Well, you know Emily won't let it go. She's going to want to investigate," I remind Andrew of Emily's tendencies.

"And you?" Andrew reminds me of *my* tendencies as he cocks an eyebrow.

I laugh. "I always lean on the side of caution."

"To stay here then." It's not a question.

"Well, I was gonna say keep a close eye on them."

"That's surprising," Andrew chuckles.

"What makes you think that?" I ask.

"Please, don't take offense. It's just you worry an awful lot about us and... and…"

"Andrew. Just say it." I roll my eyes.

"It's a good thing when you think about it, but sometimes you're just a little too cautious about things. You're like our leader, but I think sometimes you just have to take a chance. So yeah, I thought you would have stayed away, especially after how everything turned out these last few days. Looks like I would have lost more money that I don't have if I were a betting man," Andrew laughs.

"Hilarious," I say, punching him in the shoulder. "It's just that I feel like I have to protect you and Emily. So, yeah, I guess I'm a little cautious. Sue me. And, for the record, I think keeping an eye on a potential threat is leaning to the side of caution."

"I guess you've had it right all along," Andrew laughs.

"You better believe it." I smile. After getting to my feet, I reach down and help him up. I give him a side hug. "Thanks for being honest with me."

We head back to our room, Starsky limping at our heels. As we get to the door, it flies open and Emily storms out. She stomps across the hall to Carissa's door, and with a fist, she pounds on it, and waits for it to open with her hands on her hips. The door opens as if Carissa is afraid of what's waiting on the other side. Emily spits, stamping out each word, "Your training begins tomorrow. We can't afford to have you as a liability. Make sure you're dressed in something other than that." She points to Emily's dress and fancy shoes. "And make sure you do something with your hair."

Carissa stands there, her mouth agape, as Emily turns around and walks back towards us. Andrew and I stare at her in amazement as she approaches. She stops and raises an eyebrow, "What? I was nice." Then she walks past us and into the room, closing the door.

We look back at Carissa whose mouth still hasn't closed. Andrew nods and chuckles, "She'll grow on you."

"She will, I say, trying to reassure her. "Good night." Andrew and I walk into the room and close the door.

Chapter 4

Training Begins

When I wake the next evening, Emily and Andrew aren't there. After washing my face with some cool water from the sink, I set out to find them. The hallway is dark except for a light shining through one of the laboratory windows. I can hear Emily shouting, "Let's go! Get up and do it again!"

I peek into the window. Carissa is on the floor, sweat matting her hair across her frustrated face. A broomstick sits by her side. Emily is standing over her, a broomstick in her hands, crouched in a fighting stance, determination etched into her eyes. She yells again, "How have you survived this long without knowing how to fight? Get up and do it again. Let's go. Pick up your staff. Hold it like this. One palm up. One palm down. Put your non-dominant foot facing forward and your other one pointing out like an L."

I watch Carissa, her eyes narrowed with anger, pick up the broomstick and mimic what Emily tells her. Emily walks around her and kicks Carissa's back foot to its proper place. She stands next to her so Carissa can see her. "Now," Emily demands, "with both hands on the staff, lift it over your shoulder like you're going to use an axe to chop wood." Carissa watches and tries her best to match as Emily circles her like a shark, making adjustments. "Let's try this again. We are going to do a basic combination. First will be an overhead front strike. Bring your front leg up. As you step forward, rotate your arms and the staff down as if you are hitting someone on the head with the top portion of the staff. Show me!" Carissa does it. It looks good to me, but Emily isn't impressed. "Now, with the other side of the staff, bring it down as if someone is going to strike your legs. This is how you block it. If you were in an actual fight, you can also sweep someone's leg, bringing them to the ground. Show me." Again, Carissa works through the next move. "Okay, now start from the top." Carissa performs the combination three times.

Just then, Andrew and Starsky come out of the containment room. "Oh hey, are they still at it?" Andrew asks.

Starsky trots to my side and licks my hand. I notice his limp is getting better. "How long has this been going on?"

"I watched for a while before Starsky and I went to grab a bite."

"Looks like Emily isn't going easy on her," I point out.

"You think? That's our Emily. I guess this may be her way of working through her issues with Carissa."

We turn our attention to the window again. Emily and Carissa are facing off against each other. "Don't go easy. Think about what I told you and just do it! Don't overthink it. Just do it!"

"Overhead strike and then rotate the stick down to block," Carissa talks through the steps.

"It's a staff! Not a stick."

"What difference does it make?" Carissa asks, crossing her arms in front of her in frustration.

"Every detail is important. When you are out there against those things, every detail matters. There is nothing more important than the little things. When we are all fighting together, we pay attention to every detail. Sorry this isn't a trip to the mall with your girlfriends looking at makeup or trying on cute girly clothes. This is real life! The sooner you accept it, the better. Stop being such a prima donna and *fight*!"

Carissa explodes by stepping forward and rotating the staff towards Emily's head. With precision and speed, Emily counters by bringing her staff above her head, blocking Carissa's strike. Then, Carissa rotates the bottom half of the staff to block Emily's lower strike, but Emily's too quick. Her strike upends Carissa's feet lifting her off the ground. She lands flat on her back, knocking all the air out of her lungs.

Andrew and I wince at Emily's actions. "That's gonna leave a mark," I chuckle.

"The only thing we're missing is some popcorn," Andrew laughs. "That's about the fourth time she's landed like that. It's already happened three times when Starsky and I watched earlier. She's gonna have a hard time moving tomorrow."

Starsky whines, wanting to go into the room with Emily. Andrew looks down at him. With a raise of his eyebrow, Starsky stops. Andrew nods his head, and Starsky backs up a few steps and sits down.

As I glance back to Starsky, Carissa's voice breaks in, "Why do you have to act like that!?"

Emily stands over Carissa, "Act like what!?"

"Like that! You're the meanest person I've ever met! No matter what I do, no matter what I say, it's never good enough for you! You're seriously a jerk!"

"Oh, really? Coming from you, that's almost a compliment!" Emily shouts, her eyes fixed on Carissa's.

"Is that what this is about? So much for trying to work things out. Isn't that what you said, Emily? I already told you my father had gone mad, and I just did what he told me to do. I never realized it would go that far!" Andrew and I shoot surprised glances as Carissa grabs her staff and gets to her feet, and although she keeps a safe distance away, stands with squared shoulders opposite Emily. "How many times do I have to say it?"

"That's not what this is about," Emily stamps. I'm surprised by her response. It's the perfect time for her to confront Carissa about how she's feeling. Instead, she sidesteps the conversation and makes it about something else. "Kieran and Andrew and I have survived this long by counting on each other and getting better at survival. You? You wouldn't survive five minutes on your own."

"Yeah. It's hard to miss that point, seeing how you already brought it up like a million times!"

"Because it's important! When we are in the heat of battle, we know we can rely on each other. You? You have no skills. No prowess. No will to fight. If you went into battle with us, not only would we have to worry about the Feasters, we'd have to protect you because you can't even protect yourself! You are a liability! Because of you, we would run the risk of someone getting hurt or worse… bitten! That's why I'm a jerk!"

"I'm not like you. I don't have Vampire powers. But I'm not helpless!"

"Oh, really? You think being a Vamp has something to do with it? I've taught myself these skills because we have to survive. If not, then we become meals for the Feasters! What skill set could you possibly have to help us in a fight? Oh, I know. I bet you were a cheerleader, right? Are spirit fingers going to take down a zombie?" Imitating a cheerleader, Emily claps her hands together and squares her shoulders. "I'm right, aren't I?"

Carissa narrows her eyes, insulted, and her face grows red at Emily's words. Tears come to the corners of her eyes. "I was a cheerleader, and I was good!"

"So what if you were good? It's still not going to help us."

"I was more than just that. I was a flyer!"

Emily furrows her eyebrows, "What the heck is a flyer?"

Carissa throws down her staff and stomps out of the laboratory and out into the hallway. She doesn't even acknowledge us. Emily watches from the window as Carissa walks down the hallway several steps and turns around to face us. After taking a deep breath, she runs and performs two front handsprings, finishes with a forward flip, and sticks the landing. After a moment to catch her breath, she turns around and walks back to face Emily. She slaps the window and yells through the glass, "I'm not helpless. You'll see! I'll prove it to you." Her voice cracks. She storms down the hallway, limping and holding her back, aching from her training with Emily, to her room for the evening.

The three of us look at each other through the glass. I smile and admit, "She might be alright after all."

Andrew chuckles, watching Emily's shocked face as she picks up the broom sticks and exits the room. Without a word, she brushes past us and heads to the containment room.

Andrew and I turn to follow. When we get to the door, I notice Andrew looking back at Starsky, who is still sitting where we were watching Emily and Carissa train. He locks his gaze with Starsky's pleading eyes. Andrew deliberately blinks his eyes, and Starsky hustles to his side. "Okay," I say. "What's going on? That's the second time I've seen Starsky do something by you just looking at him."

He claps me on the back and says, "It's nothing. Ole Starsky and I have been doing a little training." He scratches the top of the German Shepherd's head.

"After one day?"

"What can I say? He's a quick learner." With that, he and Starsky walk into the containment room.

Emily's slurping fills the room as she nourishes on one of the pigs. Starsky sprawls out pawing at one of Big Bertha's legs, laying in the corner while Andrew and I wait for Emily to finish. When she does, she says, "Why are you guys being so weird?"

Andrew chuckles, "You're being weird." He makes a silly face at her by sticking out his tongue and crossing his eyes.

"Real mature," she smirks back, wiping the blood off her lips with the back of her hand while retracting her fangs.

"So, how's the training going?" I ask, wondering what she thinks about Carissa's skills. "Is she picking it up?"

"Ha!" Emily laughs. "She may pick up the moves, but she doesn't have a killer instinct. I spent over an hour teaching her basic moves, and she couldn't do it. I even got under her skin and tried to make her mad so she would dig deep and do something."

"She gave it a go the last time, right?" Andrew asks.

"She's sooo slow," Emily complains, moving her arms as if in slow motion. "I mean, yeah, she got the move right, but we worked on that same move repeatedly. She knew what to expect and still couldn't stop it," Emily teases.

"That last time she took a good swing at you. Lucky for you, you're quicker, or she would have broken your nose," Andrew laughs.

"That would be a shame on such a pretty face." Andrew smolders a look at Emily, making her blush.

"Ha! Like she ever could," Emily laughs. "And, yes, I have a pretty face, and it's way out of your league. Thanks for noticing, though." She recovers from her embarrassment over Andrew's flirting.

"That cheerleading comment really got to her," I say.

"No doubt, she had to be good at it," Andrew points out. "That flipping thing she did in the hallway was pretty impressive."

"My guess," I add, "is that she got teased or labeled in school. It makes sense. She was pretty sensitive about it. How did you figure her to be a cheerleader?"

"That? Easy. I've always found myself easily annoyed by the type. You know, a fake kind of peppy. Always flirting. Always getting their way." Andrew and I shoot each other glances. Emily notices, "What?"

"Sounds like something personal happened," Andrew says.

"Well, let's just say I didn't have the best rapport with them. They always just glared at me in school, thinking because they have friends, they were better than me."

"We're Vamps. Everyone glared at us," I point out.

A contemplative silence settles in for a moment before Andrew asks, "Was it really bad for you guys? I mean, we've never talked about it before."

I sigh, "Bad. I mean horrible. The constant battle of dealing with being bullied and picked on crushed my spirit. They never accepted us. It helped when my parents took me out of school and taught me at home, but it never healed those wounds."

"And the stares. The constant stares. I never understood how people figured us to be Vamps. I mean –,"

"It's your eyes and posture," Andrew interrupts.

"What?" Emily and I ask, confused.

"It's your eyes and posture."

"Yeah, you've already said that," Emily answers, scratching the ear of one pig who nudges her hand, encouraging it for more.

"It's how Vamps walk or move. I don't know. There's something about how you carry yourselves. A certainty in your eyes. Like a controlled confidence which warns, no matter how bad things get, you can take over. I think it's what's always kept humans at bay and probably the reason why Vamps were never fully accepted before the Feasters. I'm guessing it's the reason Harold tried to, ya know, eradicate us. Yeah, it's definitely those things. I've been a Vamp for a year, and I don't think I have the confidence yet."

"Well, whatever it is," Emily adds, "there are times I'm glad the Feasters took over. We don't have to deal with all of the looks anymore. I've almost never felt freer from their stares and the judgment and the fear. I hated that."

"Well, I have mixed feelings about it since pretty much everybody I knew was human," Andrew admits.

"Oh, I'm sorry," Emily regrets, realizing her words, which for Emily is an enormous step in the right direction. "That was insensitive. I didn't mean it that way. I sometimes forget. Those memories burn deep."

Andrew runs his fingers through his black hair. "I get it. I miss my family," Andrew confides, tears pooling in his eyes. "You know, my parents were never like the others."

"The others?" I ask.

"Like those humans that made you feel insignificant. My parents were hippy-types. They thought everyone was equal regardless of race, gender, or species. They became so frustrated whenever some kind of injustice happened on TV. They would spend hours explaining to me the importance of judging a person's actions and what they do for others. Not by their color and stuff like that."

"Did you listen to them?" Emily asks.

"Ha, of course I did. Why do you think I didn't freak out when I found out you changed me? At first, I was super mad, but after hearing your reasoning, I thought better. I mean, you saved my life."

"Did you ever have friends like us? Vamps?" I ask.

"I didn't have many friends at all. People thought I was weird."

"Well, that's not a shock," I joke.

"Ha ha, ya jerk. There were only a few people I could call my friends. One of them was a Vamp. She did everything she could to blend in. She wanted so badly to come to school, so she covered from head to toe to protect her skin. But she got picked on all the time. I endured my fair share of black eyes defending her. So, yeah, I got to witness a bit of what you guys have been through."

"A girl?" Emily asks. She fails to hide her jealousy and curiosity.

"Yup. A girl. A Vamp girl. I guess I've always had a thing for Vamp girls," Andrew eggs on recognizing Emily's discomfort. I'm trying so hard to keep from laughing. These two. I seriously love them together.

Andrew and I look at each other and can no longer contain ourselves, and we bust out laughing. Emily shoots us stern glances before the corners of her mouth curl up. "Honestly," she muses, "you guys are such jerks."

Andrew shoots a smile at Emily, followed up by a wink, "Emily. No other girl could ever grab a hold of my heart the way you have."

Redness fills Emily's cheeks again. Noticing this, I bail her out and change the subject, "So, I've been having some dreams."

Emily rights herself, "Oh really?"

"Yeah, well, it's been just one dream. I've had fragments over the past couple of nights. But last night, I had the whole dream."

"What about?" Andrew asks.

"It's about that night the Feasters took over. Remember it, Emily?"

"How could I forget?" Emily questions, but it's more of a statement.

"My dream takes place the night right before they forced us upstairs. I'm sure we've talked to you about this, Andrew. After we lost all communication with the outside world, our family tried to do something about the Feasters. Because it was too dangerous outside, we'd hid in our houses for days. Our elders assumed what made us physically superior as Vamps could help to make some headway getting rid of them. They were wrong. They were so wrong. When our family went out there, we had no effect at all. No matter how many times our kind bit them, it did nothing but give those monsters an opportunity to gnaw on their flesh. The ones who couldn't make it into the house lay on lawns and sidewalks. Our family converted the living room into a makeshift triage and did their best to treat the many bite wounds. Then, that evening, as if coordinated, the injured changed into them."

"I remember you telling me how your cousin bit your aunt."

"He wasn't the only one. They all changed at once and attacked us. Before we knew it, we had to hide upstairs while the chaos unfolded."

The three of us reflect on all we've lost. Emily asks, "So, what happened in your dream? Another warning?"

"A warning? It could have been. I can't be too sure. Maybe." I run the dream over in my mind. "You and I were sitting on the stairs in shock looking over our family tending to the wounded."

"I remember that and praying to God to make it all go away."

"We all were," I say, nodding my head. "There was something different in my dream."

"What's that?" Emily asks.

"I had this feeling that my mother was there."

"Aunty? That is strange," Emily notes.

"Why strange?" Andrew asks, confused.

"My mother died in an accident several years *before* the Feasters outbreak."

"Oh, you never talked about how before. I mean, of course, I don't blame you."

I nod my head, "Yeah, so it was so odd to feel her there. There were sounds too. I heard a song playing in the background. I'm not even sure why it's important, but it won't leave my memory. It felt familiar."

"Well, your parents always had music playing in their house. It was kinda nice, I remember," Emily reminisces.

"There was something else. I heard some kind of tapping. I left you on the stairs to search for it. As I moved around the room between all the injured, the growing sense of her presence mounted into my consciousness. She had to be there, and the tapping sound would lead me to her."

"Well, did you find her?" Emily asks.

"Yes, but it wasn't pretty. I parted the curtains covering the front window. Her face was bloodied. She began banging like her life depended on it and shouting, 'He's not dead! He's not dead!' That's when I saw Stevie attack Aunt Gigi. Both times I woke up."

"Wow! That's heavy. Sorry you had to have *that* dream," Andrew acknowledges.

"So, what do you think it all means?" Emily asks.

"I don't know. It's not like my usual dreams where there's some kind of warning about the future, something cryptic. But this time? My mother warned me about something which already happened. It made no sense."

"Bizarre," Emily admits.

"Yeah, it could just be my brain making sense of what's happened this past week."

"It has been pretty crazy," Andrew snickers.

I'm cautious about every dream now more than ever. It would be helpful if they came with interpretation. Since they don't, I will have to hold Emily and Andrew close and look for signs to understand them.

Chapter 5

Carissa

I wake up earlier than everyone this evening, thankful I didn't dream. Being open with Emily and Andrew did the trick, lifting a weight off my shoulders. Out in the hallway, there's a light coming from the laboratory. As I peek in, Carissa is rehearsing the self-defense moves Emily taught her. With the shaky precision of a novice who is still trying to gain muscle memory, she brings the staff over her head and cuts through the air and then sweeps the other end of the staff down for an invisible block. Repeatedly, she works through the steps until sweat beads on her brow.

I debate whether I should go in and offer her some tips, but also check in with how she's feeling. As I'm deciding to grab some breakfast, Carissa notices me in the hallway. She moves to the door, "Oh, hey, Kieran. I didn't realize it was you. I'm waiting for Emily."

"Yeah, people are always mistaking me for her." Carissa gets a bewildered look on her face, trying to make sense of what I said. I let it sit for a moment before bailing her out. "Carissa, I'm kidding."

She pauses a moment, "Oh! I was thinking you and Emily don't even look alike. I can be so naïve sometimes." We both laugh.

"Do you know how to do all this stuff?" She asks, holding the staff in her hand as if she's ready to fight and a smile plastered across her face.

"I've learned a thing or two along the way."

"Do you think you could teach this girl that thing or two?" Her deep brown doe eyes flutter in a way which catches me off guard.

"Uh, sure. I guess. Emily is the real master at all this. But I guess I can show you what I know."

I follow her into the room. She stops, causing me to bump into her, "What's with her!? I mean, nothing I do. Nothing I say. And, believe me, I've been trying. But, nothing is good enough for her."

I nod my head. "Carissa, I think she's having a hard time processing all of this. Of the three of us, she's the most headstrong. With all the stuff with your dad and almost losing Andrew, she's struggling." I allow that to sink in for a moment before continuing, "You know the night when everything fell apart? Her mother, my Auntie Rosemary, sacrificed her life to save us. So, every time she takes out a Feaster, it's personal. Every time a Feaster gets close to biting Andrew or me, it's personal. And now, Emily's processing everything with you and your dad, Sebastian Labs and the cure. It became real. And to her, she can finally put a face to the apocalypse. It's all confusing. She'll move past this at some point, but believe me, she's going to have to do it at her own pace. And it's going to come with some bumps and bruises."

"You're telling me." Carissa manages a smile while rubbing the small of her back. She scratches her head and wrinkles her nose, thinking about what I've told her. "You know, I've realized none of that. Believe me, none of this was expected to happen."

"I believe you. How could you know?"

"My father lost his mind after Case bit my mother," Carissa says as her eyes tear up. "I never shared my father's feelings about you... about Vampires." A tear trail streams down her cheek as she lets out a loud sniffle, causing her cheeks to get flushed.

I stand up straight and tease, "What in the world was that?!"

Embarrassed, her face turns red, and this time she snorts. Her eyes widen as a snot bubble appears for a second from her left nostril before she sniffs it back up. "What the heck is happening to me?" She wipes her face on her sleeve and tries to cover up her embarrassment.

Carissa doesn't know me well enough to know I won't let this go. It's too easy. "Were you drowning a duck?! What did that poor duck do to you?"

"Oh my gosh! You are such a jerk!" Carissa laughs a flirty laugh, catching me off guard. "Seriously, a jerk!"

"That's just part of being in this family." An awkwardness fills the space between us. I'd always thought Carissa was pretty, but until now, I hadn't noticed how beautiful she is despite everything that's happened. I redirect the conversation. "Carissa, in all seriousness, I don't believe you share the same views as your father. You don't have to convince me. Or Andrew. Deep down, I don't think Emily believes it either. I just think with her, you're going to have to prove yourself along the way."

"Well, I guess so," Carissa agrees, casting her eyes downward. I turn to walk out of the room and Carissa stops me, "Hey, where are you going?"

"I'm going to get a bite to eat and let you practice," I say, trying to be cool.

"I thought you were going to show me a thing or two," Carissa smirks and shoots a flirty wink.

"Oh yeah," I comment, knowing a crimson color paints my cheeks, but I don't even bother to hide it. Instead, I do my best to roll with it and grab the staff. "Okay, let's see your moves." Carissa lifts the staff up like Emily taught her. She runs through the movements, crisper that I'd seen before. "Not bad. Can I offer some advice?"

"Of course."

"Yesterday, you did that nifty cheerleader flippy thing in the hallway."

Pretending to be exasperated, she questions as if bothered, "Nifty cheerleader, flippy thing? Seriously? It's more than just a thing. I worked hard to pull *that* off. Lots of sweat. Lots of tears. And, I may or may not have broken my arm. That flippy thing is a round-off back handspring. So, what about it?"

"Well, sooorry," I say, adding my own dramatics. "When you are fighting and learning how to defend yourself, use what you know to your advantage."

"How do you mean?"

"It turns out Andrew was one heck of a baseball player. So, he knows how to swing a bat. Emily took up archery on vacation, and she's been fanatical about it ever since. She worked every day to get better at it. So, take what Emily taught you and add your back hand-springy thing," I say it wrong on purpose to dig at her.

"But I need my hands to flip."

"Sounds like you are going to need some kind of harness to keep the staff strapped to your back, and then you can bring it down when you land. Wham!" I bring the staff I'm holding down.

"A harness? Like the one Andrew has for his bat?"

"Something like that. You'll figure it out. Keep practicing. Show Emily you want to be part of our family." Carissa reflects on this for a moment. "Look, I am starving. Plus, I'm sure Emily's up by now. You should get practicing."

Carissa calls to me as I walk out of the room, "Hey Kieran?"

"Yeah?"

"I know what Andrew and Emily used to help strengthen their fighting skills."

"Okay?"

Carissa puts her hands on her hips and tilts her head to one side, "So, what skill do you have?"

I smile and reach for the knob and say, "Me? I'm just good looking." I leave the room in disbelief of what I just said, but I own it without looking back.

For three days, Emily trained Carissa. For three days, Carissa ended up on her back from Emily's staff. For three days, Carissa, injured and sore, continued to train on her own to prove her place to Emily. On the fourth day, Carissa's training paid off. Well... sort of.

During a time where things had become so mundane, Emily's training sessions turned into a needed distraction. Andrew and I would wake up early so we wouldn't miss any of the action. Over the course of the three days, something changed inside Carissa. She still needs more practice, even though she swings the staff with a little more precision. She still takes a steady beating during Emily's training. In fact, Emily insists on turning up the pressure. However, a steady boil builds inside her each time she picks herself up after her body hits the ground. And like an overly full pot of boiling water, it bubbles over.

As we watch from the window, Emily just knocked Carissa down for the fourth time. This time Carissa, with a fire burning in her eyes, stands up. She seems to fend off any pains she may be feeling. "Again!" Carissa demands of Emily.

"You don't give up, do you?" Emily chides. "Alright, then. Let's go!" Without direction, Carissa is already in position.

"I'm done getting my butt kicked. I'm done playing the victim!" Carissa spits.

Emily smiles and lets out a quick chuckle. "Well, it's about time. If you think you can, then come get it."

Carissa places the staff in a makeshift harness on her back to free her hands. Then she takes a step back and darts towards Emily. She performs a round-off back handspring and flips over Emily. While in the air, she takes staff back into her hands and whips an overhead strike toward Emily's head, but she's too quick and blocks Carissa's attempt. In one motion, Carissa drops the backend of the staff and sweeps Emily's leg. Surprised, Emily loses her footing and lands on her back with a thud. Carissa stands over Emily staring at her staff, unbelieving of her achievement. Then all at once, it hits her. She squares her shoulder and gloats, "Ha! I did it! You said I didn't have what it took to defend myself. That's what this cheerleader can do!" Carissa throws two thumbs at herself. As the words leave her mouth, an angry Emily reacts, swinging her staff at Carissa's ankles, knocking her down again. The two girls lay on their backs, side-by-side, panting. Without looking at Emily, Carissa admits, "I hate you."

After a few moments, both girls laugh and struggle to catch their breath. Emily points out, "Well, it took you long enough. I mean seriously, I pushed every stupid button I could to get you to be angry enough to get you out of your head."

"You were just getting under my skin?"

"Well, don't get me wrong, I'm still not sure about you or... even like you, but if you are going to be with us, I have to know that we can trust you when the going gets tough. When our lives are on the line. Let's just call tonight a good start."

Silence rests between them. Then Carissa sits up, looking at the blisters on her hands from days of training. "You know, I'm holding onto so much regret... about everything. I was serious when I said my father had gone mad and things weren't supposed to turn out the way they did. It all unraveled after Case was bitten." Emily locks eyes with Carissa, likely reliving all that's happened to us because of Harold. It's when Emily lowers her glare, Carissa confesses, "I have nightmares about him."

"About who?" Emily asks, confused.

"My brother. Case. Of all of us, he deserved none of this, especially being turned into one of them."

I can see Emily is holding back and trying to play nice. She chooses her words with care and delivers them less like she's breaking a bottle on the ground. "None of us deserve this, Carissa."

"I guess, but I don't think you *really* believe that," Carissa presses.

Emily cocks her head. "Well, I didn't want to bring that up."

"It's something we can't dance around either." I listen by the door, surprised that Carissa's the one who brings this up.

"I'm not dancing around it. I hate dancing," she smirks. "Trust me, I will bring it up when I want to."

"Every conversation about my father doesn't have to be an explosion."

"I don't explode," Emily retorts and wrinkles her nose at the notion.

Carissa spins towards Emily and crosses her legs. "Really? Since moving down here to the luxurious bowels of Sebastian Labs, I feel this is the first time you haven't wanted to rip my head off or ship me out to the Feasters."

Emily, uncomfortable with the close space between her and Carissa, shifts her weight back. "When I think about all your family has done to us, believe me, it crosses my mind. First ripping off your head and then feeding you to the Feasters." To my surprise, Emily smiles for a second before it evaporates, "But, I'm working on it. I understand you are just a kid like the rest of us and if you say you didn't support your father's beliefs, then I am forced to believe it. It's just going to take some time accepting it."

"He deserved it, you know." Carissa shifts her weight, looking down towards her feet.

"Who deserved what?"

"My father. I know that sounds awful." Tears spill into her eyes. "Oh my God, it sounds terrible! I don't know who I am anymore." She manages a chuckle rooted more in embarrassment.

"No one should ever do what he did, regardless of who they are. All those Vamps in the containment room, the ones you and Kieran battled in the hallway. They were somebody. Like, someone loved them. They were part of someone's family. I just assumed… I mean, it surprised me." Carissa wipes her face with her sleeves before continuing, "To think that the man, who loved me and my brother and cared so much for my mother, was capable of such atrocities is hard to accept. His ending was fitting. And ironic, too. I don't know how many times I have to apologize, but I will keep saying it as long as I have to."

"Then, why did you go along with his plans?"

"That's a fair question, and I don't have a brilliant answer. Even though revenge consumed him, I knew my dad wanted to do the right thing. I thought he could cure my mother and maybe even Case. So, I just trusted that once he did, he would focus on saving the world somehow. I had to believe he would make the world right. It was the hope I had left."

Both girls grow quiet. Carissa's head is down, and tears drip to the floor. I know that look on Emily's face. She's conflicted because she wants to hate Carissa, but her story makes sense.

"Anyway, I still wonder about Case. I picture him walking with a bunch of strangers. I know it sounds stupid, but I get this sense he's afraid. He's looking for me. I know it's not true, but there's no one to hug him or tickle him. My heart breaks knowing he's out there roaming with them. Feeding on whatever Feasters feed on. Do you know what's funny? He was such a picky eater. I swear he wouldn't even eat pizza if the cheese was still on it," she chuckles, looking into the air as if she's picturing him. "Anyway, I'm so thankful you and Kieran didn't let him burn in that fire." She pauses, likely thinking about happier times with Case. "I feel, as the only one left in my family, I need to go out there and finally lay him to rest."

"Besides having to end your mother and father, have you ever had to kill a Feaster before?" Emily asks.

"Just one. The day a Feaster bit Case."

"Where did that happen?"

"Back at the house, over a year ago. Like everyone else, we went into lockdown. Father secured the house so nothing could get inside. He wanted to make sure we were safe alone, so he could clean up the mess Sebastian Labs caused. He felt obligated to spend more time there to help stop the spread of the infection."

"So, was the house not secure? Did the Feasters get inside?"

"Quite the opposite. It was like Fort Knox."

"So what happened?" Emily focuses, intent on hearing the story.

"One afternoon, my mother took a nap which, given the monotony, happened often. Every day blended into the other. Sleep schedules didn't exist. Well, I was in charge of Case while she slept. From a very young age, he earned the name Houdini. You know, after the famous magician? No crib or playpen or gate would keep him in or out. He always found a way. Like any six-year-old, Case loved to play outside and being contained inside drove him crazy. So, Little Houdini did what he did best. He found a way out through the garage by piling up some milk crates and unlocking the deadbolts my father installed. Sure enough, he found his way into the backyard."

"Where were you?" Emily asks with more interest than accusation.

"I went up to my room to get something. Makeup of all things. Seriously, what normal person worries about lip gloss during the apocalypse?" Carissa's voice cracks with emotion. "I left him putting together some building blocks. I didn't even notice he wasn't there when I returned. Well, not until I heard him scream. Panicked, I jumped up, looking around for him. When he screamed a second time, I knew he wasn't in the house. I raced to the back window and saw him on the ground. One of them knelt over his body, face bloodied. Without thinking, I grabbed the bat we kept next to the door, unlocked the deadbolt locks, and raced out to save my brother! When I approached the zombie," Carissa said, tears streaking through the sweat stains on her face, "I swung that bat like my life depended on it —"

"Because it did!" Emily interrupts, eyes captivated in Carissa's story.

"— and I didn't stop swinging at his skull even after it broke open until my mother grabbed me. I froze in her arms, gathering my senses. When we both looked down at Case, his insides were torn into.

Dropping beside his body, I spun into my mother's arms, sobbing and screaming. Still secured in her hug, her grip tightened around me. 'Carissa. Look,' my mother said. Case's fingers slowly folded and unfolded. My mother let go of me and lifted Case's body onto her lap.

"'Mother?'" I asked, "'Is – Is he alive?'" Case's eyelids fluttered. My dread turned to hope. Hoping he was going to be okay. Hoping I could hear him laugh again. But my hope faded fast because when Case opened his eyes, he turned into..." Carissa pauses as emotion washes over her, holding her underwater so the next words can't come out.

"One of them? A Feaster?" Emily asks, already knowing the answer but enthralled in the story.

Carissa nods her head, shaking her hands to collect herself. "His eyes," Carissa tries to shake the image from her mind. "A fog covered his eyes. I couldn't even see their color. He looked up towards my mother with rage and chomped at the air between them, hoping to taste her flesh. My mother dropped him on the ground and pulled me upwards. Case lay there for a second, which left me wondering if we were just seeing things. But then all at once, he sat up as if lifted like a puppet on strings. In slow motion, he turned to us and struggled to his feet. Conflicted, my mother pulled my arm, and we ran. We ran, Emily. We ran from my brother. Neither of us knew what to do. For hours, we watched in disbelief as he wandered around the backyard as if our house was still familiar to him. Like at any moment, he'd walk through the back door and ask me to play something with him."

"What about the basement?" Emily asks. As I'm listening, the image of Case floods forward to my mind, his boyish stature encapsulated in the body of a Feaster. In the two years since the outbreak, his image was the most difficult to see and twists my stomach into sadness.

Carissa continued, "The next day, my father returned home. He built that cage in the basement. Then, with all the courage he could, he walked outside, sedated Case, and locked him down there."

Emily stared at Carissa in disbelief. Then, she lowered her head as the story weighed heavy on her, too. "Whoa, so you've been through a lot more than I give you credit for. That sounds brutal. I had no idea," Emily admits, putting her hand onto Carissa's.

"The worst part of this is that it was all my fault. Case's turning. My mother's depression. Her death. My father's death. All of it. I carry it with me every single minute of every single day. If I had just done what they expected of me; watch the greatest little guy of all time, none of that would have happened. My parents never said they blamed me, but they didn't have to. I could see it in their eyes. Anytime my parents mentioned his name, or we could hear him growling from the basement, they'd shoot quick glances in my direction. When my mother became distraught, she would sit down there for hours reading to him and trying to be a mother. It was because of me. My selfishness. I will never forgive myself." Emily moves next to Carissa and puts her arms around her. For minutes, Carissa heaves sobs into Emily's shoulder.

In the hallway next to the opened door of the laboratory, Andrew, Starsky, and I sit with our backs against the wall, awestruck at this revelation. It's true, Carissa had been through as much as we had. We underestimated that. This may be the thing Emily needs to understand Carissa and move forward in accepting her. I look down at Starsky and he moves to Andrew's lap as if sensing his emotions.

From inside the laboratory, Emily stands up and offers her hand to Carissa, which she takes. Once on her feet, Emily offers, "Hey, if you need to talk about this again, you can talk with me. Girl to girl."

"That would be awesome. I guess you aren't so awful after all," she chuckles, unsure how her attempt at a joke is going to go over.

Emily laughs, "Don't be too sure. I can be pretty moody."

Carissa acts as if she's surprised about this. "Shut up! You? C'mon."

"Watch it, missy."

Carissa smiles. "It was nice talking with you. You're always so darn scary most of the time. It's nice to see this side of you."

"It's nice to have a girl to chat with, I guess. Those goofs sitting out in the *hallway* don't know how to talk to a *girl*!" Emily blurts out so we can hear her.

"Oh snap, we're busted!" Andrew whispers loudly as we freeze in place.

Emily cocks her head and makes her eyebrows dance up and down. "I'm starving. I'm going to join those knuckleheads."

"Yeah, and I'm exhausted."

As both girls exit the room, Emily turns to Carissa and admits, "That little flippy thing was pretty cool. You almost got me."

Carissa laughs, "It's not a flippy thing." She stops herself. "Never mind. I'm going to bed." She smiles at us and heads to her room.

"You guys are such knuckleheads," Emily chirps, walking across the hallway.

"What?" Andrew poorly attempts to play off we weren't eavesdropping.

"I could hear you breathing. You're like a stupid pug dog. The ones with the smashed up faces that grunt whenever they breathe or get excited."

"Speaking of smashed faces, Carissa almost smashed yours," I say, poking fun.

"Like she could. What you should be talking about was my incredible overhead block," Emily boasts.

"Um, what we should talk about is how Carissa did the nifty leg sweep with the staff and knocked the great Emily Estrie flat on her back," Andrew jokes, expecting Emily's wrath at any moment.

To my surprise, she doesn't defend herself other than to say, "That won't happen again. I don't let my guard down in battle. No distractions other than kicking butt." She nods her head and gloats, "She's getting better. I'd say she's my greatest accomplishment." Entering the containment room, Emily sits next to one pig. "Maybe one day, I can even teach you to fight," she jokes, scratching the pig behind its ear before biting down on its vein.

"Sounds like Carissa's been through a lot. More than any of us ever realized," I say, wondering everyone's thoughts.

"The story about Case was tough to listen to. Poor little guy," Andrew recalls, shaking his head in disbelief.

"I know it sounds crazy, but I'm even more comfortable letting him out of that cage before we burned Harold's house to the ground," I say, thinking about the last time I saw his silhouette outside the gates of the place he once played games and felt love. Listening to Carissa's story immersed me in memories of my family. The laughter and connection. The love. I don't allow myself the luxuries of those memories very often because the pain is too great.

Each of us finishes our meals. I reminisce about my family. Each memory is categorized in good times and bad times. Things weren't always perfect, but I miss all of it. I am thankful for the family I have right here. Emily and Andrew. They are my source of strength when I am lacking hope. Now, it looks as if Carissa is learning to find her place among us. In time, she may even be part of this family.

As I look over the room, two of the pigs and Starsky are laying in front of Andrew as if they are attending school, like they are waiting for him to say something. Andrew transfers a soft gaze onto each of them. Then, he closes his eyes and each of the animals rests their heads on the ground. I look over at Emily and her mouth is open in astonishment.

"Okay, seriously, what is going on with the animals, Andrew?" I ask.

Andrew opens his eyes and beams from ear to ear. "You really wanna know?"

Chapter 6

Andrew's Gifts

All naturally born Vampires possess some sort of special gift aside from common ones such as strength, speed, and conditional immortality. Our ancestors believed these gifts had evolved after many generations. They manifest in different ways. Dreams are my gift, though I don't always see it this way. Sometimes it feels like a curse. Sometimes it's a cruel friend who holds secrets and leaves you wondering if you are worthy enough for them to let you in on the juicy details. Meanwhile, they keep you guessing if the secret they're holding so close is about you. In the lottery of Vampire gifts, I'd say I didn't hit the jackpot. But my dreams aren't always bad. Often, they are warnings. Sometimes, they're straightforward, where I can determine meaning. For the more complex dreams, there are few Vampires who can interpret them. Even then, there is no guarantee for perfect interpretation. My parents used to reassure me that my gift of dreams is truly a wonder and highly regarded in the Vampire world.

Emily's gift is a little more straightforward. She gets what she calls the tingles. It's a much more useful gift than dreaming. The tingles are this sense that something is wrong. It's very superhero-like.

Whenever things don't feel right, she gets these pinpricks on the back of her neck. Her tingles have saved our butts several times.

For those turned into a Vampire, it's a different story. Sometimes they're gifted powers and sometimes, well, they get just the speed, strength, and conditional immortality part. Healing is always slower, and if a wound is life threatening, it's a race against time. Andrew never fully recovered from his leg injury when Emily found him hiding in the closet. Blood poisoning and infection crept into his body. By the time Emily turned him, his leg had been damaged for too long, leaving him with a slight limp. For those who are lucky enough to gain gifts, they can differ from Vampire to Vampire. Some get agility. Others get an extra dose of strength. I've even heard stories of Vampires being able to see through walls. It looks like Andrew's gift took a year to develop.

"So, a couple of months ago, I started hearing what I thought to be voices," Andrew explains, leading Emily and me out into the hallway.

"Ha," I say to Emily, "I told you he was crazy. You owe me five bucks."

"I'm pretty sure I guessed that long before you did," Emily replies with a goofy smile.

Before I could respond with a chuckle, Starsky nips at my jeans. Emily and I stare down in astonishment. "What the heck, Starsky? I thought you liked me." Emily and I look up to find Andrew leaning against the wall, one leg crossed in front of the other like a

Greaser from the 1950s movies my parents loved. "Wait, did you do that?" I point from Andrew to Starsky and back to Andrew.

He smiles the same easy smile Emily's grown fond of over the last year. "Do what?"

"Get Starsky to bite my butt," I respond, my voice incredulous and disbelieving.

Andrew throws his hands in the air and laughs, "What? How could I possibly have done that?" Then Starsky does it again, causing me to jump a step forward. "Man, Kieran, old Starsky there must really not like you. What did you do, steal some of his kibble?"

Emily stands next to me in disbelief. When she gathers herself, she asks, "You're totally doing that! How?"

"Do it again and I'm gonna have to tackle you," I say, rubbing my backside.

Starsky locks eyes with Andrew. When he nods his head, Starsky trots around Andrew and sits down on his left.

Emily and I lock eyes in disbelief and together we turn our heads to look back at Andrew. Emily starts, "What in the world?"

"You aren't the only ones with gifts," Andrew smiles a flirty smile at Emily.

"How long has this been going on?" I ask.

Andrew looks upwards, collecting his thoughts. "It started six or seven months ago. Small at first. Every once in a while, I'd catch one of the animals: Ms. Pickles, Starsky or Hutch, and even the goat, staring at me as if they were waiting for something. I never could figure it out. It felt as if they were trying to connect with me, like they were waiting for me to say something."

"Say something?" Emily asks. "Like tell them to sit or stay?"

"Well, not say something," Andrew shakes his head as though he's trying to put into words what he means. "It's like thoughts. Now and again, I get a sense they understand my thoughts or feelings. Sadness. Happiness."

"Like mind reading?" I ask, also trying to wrap my head around this.

"Yeah, I guess. Kinda. But it was fleeting. I'd feel it one day and then not again for a few days or even weeks. But now? Since getting kidnapped by Harold, and you know, almost dying, it's pretty constant. Those pigs? They are always waiting for me to tell them something. It's so weird."

"And Starsky?" Emily asks.

"Yup! But it comes across as far less desperate than the pigs," Andrew snickers. "Besides, he's a lot cuter than Big Bertha." Starsky nudges into his hand, requesting a scratch.

"So, what else can Starsky do?" Emily asks. "Can he rub this knot out of my shoulder? It's been hurting me since Carissa swept my leg and I landed on my back."

"Okay, check this out!" Andrew walks over to both containment rooms and opens the doors.

"Dude, if those chickens come out, it's going to take us forever to get them back in."

The pigs and the chickens trickle out into the hallway. Starsky follows the chickens, sending most of them into a flurry, and they scatter. The pigs move about in their own way. Big Bertha finds a place and lays down. Andrew moves to the center of the hallway, and like Moses himself, he raises his arms up. One by one, each chicken, pig, and even Starsky lift their heads as if to acknowledge him. As he puts his arms down, all the animals line up single file and walk towards him. He nods his head, and they stop. Andrew takes a moment and appears satisfied with the astonished looks on our faces. Then, he cocks an eyebrow up and one by one, each animal turns to file into their containment rooms. To top it off, once the pigs are in theirs, Big Bertha pushes the door closed.

I can no longer contain my excitement. "Andrew! That's incredible! I mean, seriously, you can literally talk to animals. It's more like a superpower."

"Is it like that all the time?" Emily asks.

"I'd say most of the time. The problem is it doesn't have an off switch. At least with you, Kieran, your dreams come when you sleep. Emily, your tingles show up whenever there's danger. Imagine it never turning off? There's no switch for me. They won't stop,"

Andrew chuckles more to himself. "It's like having that friend you appreciate, but once in a while, you wish they would stop talking."

"So, they communicate with you? Like tell you their thoughts and dreams?" Emily asks, chuckling at how absurd it sounds.

"No, thank God, no. That would be a nightmare. It's more like wanting."

"Wanting? What do you mean?" I ask.

"It's like they want me to communicate with them. I can't explain the feeling, but it's there. I can also tell how they are feeling. Sad. Scared. Happy."

"Wait," Emily interrupts. "Even the chickens?"

"Well, it doesn't seem like they have emotions, but the wanting to communicate is there, for sure."

"I wondered if you would get your gifts after Emily changed you. But I gotta tell you, that's an awesome one. I've never heard of anyone who's ever had it before," I say. I'm excited for him.

"When did you plan on telling us about this?" Emily wonders.

"To be honest, I couldn't be sure what was happening. I'm still figuring it out. You gotta admit, it's pretty cool," Andrew beams from ear to ear.

"Well, we're happy for you, Andrew," Emily walks over and gives Andrew a kiss on the cheek.

Andrew blushes and wonders, "I just hope it will come in handy like your gifts. Right now, it just feels like a fun trick I'd use to impress the girls."

"Well, call me impressed," Emily smiles, pinning her hair behind her ear.

Watching Andrew share his gift with us was a pretty special thing. I know part of him has struggled with his transformation, especially finding out about Sebastian Labs' intention to eradicate Vampires and giving converted humans an opportunity to become human again. I think now he fully feels like one of us. Sure, he craves blood and has the fangs to prove it. He heals like too, and he's super-fast. Still, I think he felt as if he was an outsider looking in, so this gift of his may help him feel more equal, even though we've always felt this way about him.

Chapter 7

Something From a Dream

Tonight, a dream returns. I'm back at Emily's house on that horrible night, but this time it's different. None of my relatives are in the living room caring for injured loved ones. I search for my father, but he's not there. There is, however, someone sitting in a chair facing the window where I saw my mother pounding from the outside. As I approach, I'm taken aback because it *is* my mother. My heart pounds away in my chest. I am afraid, so afraid. In my last dream, she tried so hard to warn me about something. What was it she screamed? Oh yes. 'He's not dead!' I lack control of what happens in my dreams, like riding on a sled that is racing down a hill and never knowing if the snow will be soft like fresh powder or icy. So, I brace myself knowing to expect anything while controlling nothing. When I move around to gaze at my mother's face, I am relieved she's not the bloodied image I saw in the last dream. Instead, she sits, dressed in white, as if all is right in the world, gazing with a loving smile at a letter in her hands.

Sitting on the carpet in front of her, I cross my legs and just stare. God knows how I've missed her, longing for one more hug, one more conversation, one more reassurance everything will be okay. But, for now, I enjoy this.

It catches me off guard when she shifts her gaze to me, as if not noticing I was sitting before her. "Oh, hello Kieran," her voice echoes, reverberating off the walls, as if the sound is coming from behind me in a loud whisper. "Look at you. My Kier-Bear is all grown up."

I blush at the use of my nickname, but it feels good. "Not grown up enough to still be called Kier-Bear," I say, laughing. My voice doesn't have the same distant echo hers possesses.

"You will never be too old, my Kier-Bear."

"It feels good to hear that, Mom."

She stares at me in the loving way I've longed for. "I'm proud of the man you are becoming. Never in a million years would I ever want the world you are in now. But you, you are thriving in it," her voice echoes.

I laugh at the assumption, "Mom, I wouldn't say I'm thriving. I'm pretty sure no one is thriving."

"Well, the conditions aren't optimal, but you've kept Emily and the other boy safe. What's his name?"

"Andrew. His name is Andrew. Emily saved his life," I tell her.

"Ah, but it was you, son. You made the call. Andrew would be dead today without you. See? You are thriving, thinking on your feet, and willing to make the tough calls. I'm so proud of you." My mother notices a tear race down my cheek. "What's the matter, Kier-Bear?"

"I miss you."

"Don't cry. We will be together one day when you're called home."

"When?"

"You know this already. There's a place better than any place you could imagine. We will be there together."

"When all of this is over?" I ask.

"I don't know. What I know is right now Emily and Andrew need you. They need you here. There's something coming."

"What is it?" I ask as my stomach twists upon hearing this news.

"Time will reveal it," Mother swears, softening her stare.

I bask in the warm silence between us. My heart is full with this time we have together. This dream feels as if my mother is right here with me. I want so much to reach out and touch her hands, to know this is real. Instead, a thought races to my mind. "Mother?"

"Yes, Kier-Bear?"

"I don't know if you know this, but you were here in my last dream." I wait for her to respond. She doesn't, so I continue. "Our family tended to each other. I searched the room but couldn't find you, but I knew you had to be there. Instead, I found you outside looking in through this window," I say, throwing a thumb over my shoulder.

"Yes, because I wasn't part of that terrible day," she reminds me. "It was your memory."

"So, you know about that dream?" She nods and smiles, her eyes knowing. "Do you know all of my dreams? Are you there for all of them?"

"Not all of them."

"In this last dream, I felt like you were giving me a warning. You kept saying, 'He's not dead!' Then, Stevie bit Aunt Gigi. You tried to warn me about something I already knew had happened. So, why the warning?"

She turns the letter over in her hands several times. Behind me, the distant sounds of Feasters reverberate outside the windows. This catches Mother's attention, and she looks up, unafraid. "Kier-Bear. I wasn't talking about Stevie."

This revelation makes my stomach turn like sour milk. I ask, "Then, who were you talking about?"

The Feasters' groans grow louder, as if a herd is right outside the door. Mother shifts her attention to their calls. "Sweetheart, it's time for me to go."

"Wait! Now? Who were you talking about? Who's not dead?"

"There's no time for that. I love you. They're calling for me." She stands over me and envelopes my hand in hers. Her hand feels so warm in mine. Her breath, like a warm spring breeze, surrounds me as she kisses my forehead. "I have to go." She releases my hand and walks to the door.

"Mom, don't go out there. It's not safe. Please don't go!"

She opens the door and dozens of Feasters wait for her. "It's perfectly safe out here. I love you." As she advances through the threshold, the Feasters, groaning and popping their teeth, taste the air, all part for her and allow her to pass. As if coordinated and obedient, they all follow her down the walkway, groaning and calling me out of my dream.

I'm jolted awake. I look around the room and see Emily and Andrew still sleeping. This dream, different from any other dream I've ever had, leaves me unsettled. The smell of the perfume she used to wear lingers in the room. Who was she warning me about if it wasn't my cousin Stevie? It makes little sense to me. I sit up and realize there's something in my hand. When I look down, the letter my mother held rests in my grip. This is impossible. How did this happen? Was I able to pull something from my dream into reality? Was my mother able to give me some sort of message from beyond the grave? My hands tremble as I unfold the paper and realize it's a letter my father wrote to my mother.

My Dearest Lilith,

It's been twenty-one days, six hours, and twelve minutes since you were taken from us. Words cannot express the sadness and pain my heart has endured. I'm trying to make sense of this, but you have always been the one with the logic. The one who reminded me of the truth when I lost focus. Right now, I have no clarity. This emptiness swallows me into a hole I can't dig my way out of. The only thing that helps me to move on and find purpose is Kieran. I will continue to raise him in the way we have always talked about - with virtue and dignity.

I'm struggling right now because we know who it was that caused your passing. He's someone we've read about; talked about. Someone who is part of a bigger plan. Right now, there are only whispers, but those of us who are on the inside know the truth. He is part of the ones who are looking to change us. To get rid of us. That monster was driving under the influence when he killed you. He survived. Where's the justice? Imagine being that irresponsible, but we're the ones who are dangerous? I'm struggling, Lilith. Some of our family members are talking about revenge, about getting even. I'm running out of reasons to tell them not to. This is one of those times I need you to remind me of the truth. I know the right thing to do, but I'm not sure I agree with it. For now, I

will keep on the righteous path, but the hole in my
heart grows each day knowing he's out there, and
I will never get to hold you in my arms again.

Unique is My Dove,

Silas

I am at a loss for words. Explanation escapes me. My father shielded me from this information. Who was he referring to? He knew who killed my mother that night? What a coincidence it would be if the person who crashed their car into my mother's is someone from Sebastian Labs. Who was it? The only people I know who are connected are Carissa and Harold. It couldn't be Carissa, she's too young. So, it must be Harold, or at least someone connected to Harold. Knowing my family is this closely tied to Sebastian Labs leaves me unsettled. I need answers and I'm hoping to find them here because the other place, Carissa's house, is likely reduced to ash. During our days here, we have done little exploring. Perhaps it's time to.

Knowing there are a couple of hours left in the day, Emily and Andrew will still be sleeping. I haven't decided what I will say to Carissa if she finds me snooping around. I'm not sure she will care. Still, I creep out of the room and down the hallway past her room. There's no sight of her, and there are no lights on in the hallway except the light shining from under Carissa's door. There aren't any laboratories or containment rooms this way, just offices, a janitorial closet, an elevator, and a room which houses the generator. The first office is Administration. It's as good a place as any to start. Inside there are two cubicles and another room labeled Records. Not knowing where to start, I rummage through the desks and find there isn't much other than typical office supplies, useless computers, and files in baskets encapsulated in time as if the people who worked here expected life to continue.

The Records room is locked, but I remember seeing keys in one desk. Retrieving them, I find the one to open the door. Inside, there are several file cabinets. I unlock the first one. There are what I assume to be endless employee files. I recognize a few of the names. I remember the name Nathaniel Fargo. Harold told us when one of the vampire experiments failed and the subject turned into a Feaster, Dr. Fargo wanted to report the incident, but he had an *accident* and died. Accident, sure. The other files I recognize are of Franklin and Harold Croger. Franklin Croger, the lead scientist, quoted in the article back at our house about the Vampire Aversion Medical Program, or V.A.M.P. Andrew recognized him from the picture he stole from Carissa and Harold's house. And, of course, there was Harold. We had learned a lot about him the day he tried to take Andrew from us. Regardless, I fish out both files just in case there's anything else we need to know.

After looking through the other files, there isn't anything that gives me any understanding about the letter my mother had given me. I head out to the next set of offices on the opposite side of the hallway. One placard reads Harold Croger and the other, Franklin Croger. I decide to search Harold's office first. The door's locked and the keys don't work. I've been practicing how to control my new Vampire strength and instincts since the battle to save Andrew by taking a little time each day to summon the primal urge. It's not perfected yet, but it's there simmering under the surface, and I can get it bubbling with some concentration. With Vamp strength flowing through me, the brass doorknob buckles, and with a twist of the handle, the door opens. I jump back when I'm met with a painting of Harold and Franklin dressed in lab coats and looking smug. I sneer at the painting, thinking how badly I want to rip it off the wall. Instead, I search Harold's desk. In the file drawer in the desk, one stands out. It simply reads V.A.M.P. Placing it on the desk, I try to make sense of the protocol, the process, and the terms before me. There are diagrams and other drawings. I wish I had paid more attention in science class. I press the file closed and add it to the two other files to take with me.

Opening the opposite drawer, there's not much but some hard copies of Sebastian Lab paperwork that look meaningless. I close the drawer and notice a sound different from the other drawer. When I open it again, I tap the bottom of the drawer and locate where the hollow sound is coming from. I pull up the bottom of the drawer, revealing a secret compartment. Feeling the sweat bead on my forehead, I reach inside and pull out a dated newspaper clipping from the Babylon Chronicle with the headline - ***Fatal Crash Claims Vampire Mother/Activist***. I can hear the beating of my heart like a door knocker pounding its way out of my chest. *Thud! Thud!* Thinking about the letter my mother gave me from my dream, I'm convinced I'm supposed to find this or somehow, she led me here. I never knew of the events surrounding my mother's death. Now, here it is before me. Taking a deep breath, I sit down at Harold's desk and read.

West Babylon, NY - A 35-year-old Vampire mother died after sustaining injuries in a West Babylon crash on Tuesday evening. Witnesses say Lilith Caine was traveling northbound on Arnold Avenue when 40-year-old Franklin Croger, who was traveling eastbound on Route 109, failed to stop at the red light, sending Caine's car spinning into a spillway in front of the Sunoco Gas Station parking lot. Emergency personnel used the Jaws of Life to free Caine, but she was pronounced dead shortly after arriving at the hospital.

Police say there was no definitive answer why Mr. Croger, also taken to the hospital, failed to stop and are waiting for toxicology results to determine if he was under the influence. His injuries are not considered life threatening. Franklin Croger is a lead scientist at Sebastian Laboratories.

Lilith Caine was an activist in the community who had been a voice for Vampire rights and equality. Many saw her book, *Vampires: Myths to Sink Your Teeth Into*, as the first book of its kind to tackle the hard questions humans wanted to ask but didn't know how to get the answers. She is survived by her husband, Silas, and 10-year-old son.

I am a statue frozen with this knowledge. To read this makes my stomach ill, and I try to contain my anger. Looking down at my arms, blood races through my veins. I feel my fangs drop. My red eyes illuminate the desk, catching me off guard when I see my reflection in a framed picture of the Croger family. Grabbing for it, I snap it in my hands, crushing it like reducing a cookie to crumbs, shattering the glass. This family continues to take from me, from my family. Destruction lurks around every turn. And what do we do, promise grace and protect Carissa? I better understand Emily's frustration with accepting her. Yet, still, as I slow my breathing down and fight to return to normal, I know she should not wear the sins of her family. At times, I find this concept so difficult to accept. A warm tear streaks down my face.

I struggle to gather my composure, as I glance back into the drawer. There's another article clipping. The headline reads: ***Vampire Revenge? Sebastian Lead Scientist Found Slain.*** Placing the article on the table, I set to read it.

Babylon, NY - Sheriff's officials are investigating the death of local scientist Franklin Croger. Croger was found in the parking lot at Argyle Park. It appears he was the apparent victim of a Vampire attack. According to the victim's brother, Harold Croger, the two had been out for a jog, as they do most evenings. Franklin finished the run before his brother. When Harold Croger approached the car, he

found his brother laying on the floor "clinging to life" and there appeared to be multiple bite marks on his neck. Franklin Croger died at the scene in his brother's arms.

Last September, Croger was involved in a fatal car accident. After racing through a red light, his car collided with Vampire activist Lilith Caine. Caine succumbed to her injuries at Good Samaritan Hospital. Franklin Croger was initially booked with reckless driving and driving under the influence; however, the latter charges were later dropped after the toxicology report was inconclusive.

Croger was the lead scientist at Sebastian Laboratories. The small laboratory had gained national recognition in the last few years with some controversial medical breakthroughs. In the last few months, Sebastian Labs introduced the Vampire Aversion Medical Program (V.A.M.P.). V.A.M.P. protocol involved administering a vaccine to those who could be potentially bitten by a vampire such as police officers and other first responders. However, the most controversial piece of V.A.M.P. was the "cure" of Vampires from their genetic makeup. The purpose was to cure those humans that were already converted; however, activists cited the potential ramifications to Vampires. Officials are investigating whether revenge played a role in the homicide or if it was a random act of violence.

So, this is what Harold was talking about when he said he had to watch his brother die. Looking over the letter, a realization sweeps over my mind like an unexpected flash flood, causing my hands to tremble. My father's letter talks about our family members knowing who killed my mother and exacting their revenge. Was this that revenge? Was the newspaper on point? How much did my father know about this? The next question is a heavy weight which sinks into my stomach and sickens me. Did my father get his revenge on Franklin by killing him? I sit back in the chair, overwhelmed by this. Is it some strange coincidence the Croger family is intertwined with my own, or was this some kind of odd divine intervention?

I grab the files, the newspaper clippings, and head down the hallway back to the room. There's an hour before Andrew and Emily get up. It will give me some time to look through the files, but after reading the articles, I think I may have all the information I need. I try to sneak into the room, but Emily, who's always on her guard, wakes up. "Where were you?"

I look at her and fake a smile. "You wouldn't believe me even if I told you."

"Well, you're going to tell me anyway," she says, rubbing the sleep out of her eyes. I pull up a chair next to her bed. "So, tell me. Whatcha got?"

"I think we need to wake up Andrew. He's going to need to hear this, too."

Emily rolls her eyes. Picking up a pillow, she tosses it to where Andrew is sleeping, hitting him on the head. He jumps out of bed in a panic. Emily utters, "Hey handsome. Over here. It's just us." Starsky's hair, which a moment ago stood up, lies flat on his neck.

"Good morning. What time is it?"

"It's early," I say.

"Then, why am I awake?" he complains, laying his head on his pillow.

"You're gonna want to hear this," I say with seriousness in my voice, which Andrew understands because he gets up and sits on Emily's bed.

They look at the files and newspaper clippings, and Emily asks, "So, what's all this stuff?"

"I've done some snooping. Checking out some offices down the hall."

"What made you decide to do that?" Emily asks, her eyes furrowing, no doubt wondering why I didn't invite her.

"Well," I start, "because of this." I reveal the letter my mother gave me.

Emily takes it from my hand, unfolds it, and she and Andrew set to read it. Upon finishing, she has this confused look on her face. "Where did you find this? In the offices?"

I tighten my lips, unsure how to say it. Finally, I blurt out, "My mother gave it to me?"

"Wait. What? It makes no sense. The letter is after your mother died."

Andrew interrupts, "Hold on, guys. Catch me up."

"This is a letter my father wrote to my mother after she died. I'm not sure why he did it. I know he used to keep a journal, so maybe he wrote it to serve as some kind of therapy."

"So, what do you mean your mother gave it to you?" Emily asks, frustration and confusion in her voice.

"I don't know how, but she gave it to me. I had another dream. It took place at your house again, but this time, it was just the two of us. My mother sat in her favorite chair. The one we had back at the house. I talked with her, Emily. Like, we sat down and had a conversation. It felt real. So real."

"What did she say to you?" Andrew wonders.

"A bunch of things. You know how my dreams are sometimes warnings? She said I'm needed here. I feel like something's going to happen. Also, remember how in the past couple of dreams she kept warning, 'He's not dead!'? I asked her about it." I pause, recalling her words, remembering how real it felt to talk with her.

"And?" Emily asks, putting her hands up in frustration.

"I thought she was talking about cousin Stevie. She said she wasn't talking about him."

"Well, who was she talking about?"

"She didn't say," I say, shaking my head and running my fingers through my hair.

"Hmm," Emily says. "That's so bizarre."

"Yeah, well, it gets stranger. When she got up to leave the room, she opened the front door and Feasters were waiting for her."

"Were they wanting to attack her?" Emily asks.

"No, when she left, they moved out of her way and then followed her like she was their leader. She had no fear at all."

"So, how did you get the letter?" Andrew wonders.

"During my dream, she had it in her hand. When I woke up, it was in my hand."

"Shut up!" Emily and Andrew shout in disbelief.

"It's true. I can't explain it."

Emily composes herself and asks, "Kieran, has something like this ever happened before?"

"I would have told you if it had," I admit.

"Dude, do you know what this means?" Andrew asks, his palm resting on his forehead.

"It means I can interact with my dreams more than I ever imagined."

"I mean seriously, Kieran, I don't know how it would come in handy, but it's like stuff you watch in movies or something. It's truly a wonder," Andrew says in amazement.

"It's truly scary. That's what it is. What if I pull something else out of my dreams? Something unwanted," I say, making this realization for the first time. "That – that would be frightening."

We all sit for a minute before Emily asks, "How was it to talk with Auntie?"

My eyes tear up. "You know? It was…" I pause, looking for the correct words. The truth? I hadn't thought about it. I'm so caught up in the letter I haven't taken the time to process seeing or talking with her. "It was amazing. After talking with her, I felt as if she's in a good place. I mean, the Feaster thing was a bit unsettling, but she was at ease. I never got to say goodbye to her. One day – poof – she wasn't there. There were so many times I expected her to walk through the front door. I've always struggled with that because none of it was her fault, but a younger me didn't understand, I guess."

"I totally get it," Andrew agrees. "I never got to say goodbye to either of my parents. So, yeah, I'm with you."

Emily tries to change the topic. She's never been good at sorting out feelings. "So, what's with all the other stuff?"

"These are files on Harold and Franklin Croger."

"Who's Franklin?" Emily and Andrew ask in unison.

"Franklin Croger. Harold's brother?" I say.

"Oh yeah," Andrew exclaims, snapping his fingers. "He was the dude from that newspaper article about the cure and stuff back at the house."

"And the picture you hijacked from Carissa's," Emily reminds.

"Yup! And speaking of the cure, here's a file about it." I hand over the file.

"You *have* been busy," Emily judges, laughing a sinister chuckle.

"What about those other things?"

"Well, these are two newspaper articles I found in a secret compartment in Harold's desk."

Cocking an eyebrow, Emily states, "Looks like that guy had all sorts of secrets. Doesn't surprise me at all."

I nod my head in agreement. "Well, this is a newspaper article about my mother's car accident. You will never believe who crashed into her." I feel my heart pounding in my chest again. "Franklin Croger."

"Shut up!" Emily spits. "Like seriously, what are the odds?"

"Go figure," I say. "The article explains the entire thing. He's the one who blew through the red light."

"This is unbelievable. What about the other article?"

"I thought you'd never ask. So, as you read in the letter, members of my family may have been plotting some sort of revenge against my mother's killer. I don't know what it means, but I have my guesses," I say, putting my hands up.

"What do you mean you have your guesses?" Emily asks.

"Well, this article right here reports the murder of Franklin. It even questions the motive behind his death. The killer? A Vampire." I let it soak in before continuing. "Remember when Harold had Andrew strapped into the gurney?"

"I don't," Andrew jokes, breaking the tension.

"Well, one thing I remember is he said that we had to watch you die just as he had to watch his brother die. Guys, when Franklin died, Harold was there," I say, handing over the articles. "It's all right there."

"Whoa, I guess I understand the rage," Emily admits.

Without words, they read through each of them. Andrew looks up and wonders, "What are the odds of this just being a coincidence?"

Emily's quiet. I presume she's digesting all of this. "Emily? Thoughts?" I ask.

"I guess it can be a coincidence. But, like Andrew said. What are the odds? I wonder how much Carissa knows. Does she know about all of this?"

"I can't imagine her knowing very much. Like us, she had to be pretty young," I point out.

"True. But I think we have to ask. We need to know if she knew about any of this."

"I don't see how this changes anything. Why do we need to know so badly?" I ask.

"Kieran, we need to know for our family. For our safety. Part of Carissa becoming a part of our family is knowing we can trust her. I just feel we need to know it all. No secrets. I think it's important at the very least to know what she knows."

I pat my pant legs with my hands and stand up. "Fair enough," I say.

We head out into the hallway to look for her, expecting her to be ready for another day of training with Emily. The laboratory is dark, as is the rest of the hallway. There's no light shining from under the door of her room. "Where the heck is she?" Andrew voices the question we are all thinking.

Emily knocks on her door and waits for an answer. She opens the door and only darkness meets us. "She's not in here."

"Maybe she went to another level? Who knows what she does when we're sleeping?" I say with a half-chuckle.

"When everything was normal," Andrew starts, "my older sister always had to leave a note whenever she went somewhere like to a friend's house. Maybe she left a note."

"House," Emily announces, confusing us. She sprints to the laboratory and bolts inside. "Oh man, this isn't good," she utters with panic spilling from her voice.

"What's not good?" Andrew and I ask.

"She couldn't. She wouldn't," she mutters.

"Okay, Em. There are times I question your sanity. This is one of those times," Andrew muses.

The look on Emily's face matches the panic in her voice. "The staff and harness aren't here. There are wood shavings on the floor. She sharpened her staff."

"Emily, you aren't making any sense," I say with my voice raised, matching her panic but unsure why.

"The other day Carissa mentioned going back to the house to end her brother. Something about getting the chance to lay her brother to rest. She couldn't bear the thought of him walking around with a bunch of Feasters."

I nod my head, remembering the conversation while we eavesdropped in the hallway. Then it hits me all at once. "You don't think... do you?"

"I do. I think she went back to her house to find Case!" Emily exclaims.

"Why would she go alone?" I ask.

"She probably thinks she needs to prove herself to us," Andrew reveals. "That's my guess."

"We've got to go get her," I stamp out in urgency. We rush back to our room, gear up, and get ready. It feels like forever since I've held my machete in my hands. Spinning it in my grip, I harness it across my back. Hopefully, we won't have a fight on our hands and Carissa's safe.

Chapter 8

Remember Your Training

We clear a small group of Feasters as we exit Sebastian Labs. The minivan isn't there, confirming our suspicion Carissa left. The four of us, including Starsky, pile into the Camaro. Emily makes it come alive. "Everybody ready?" She gives it gas and the tires scream, cutting a path along the asphalt.

As we drive down towards the cul-de-sac, we see the silhouettes of a small group of Feasters moving towards what's left of Harold and Carissa's house. Emily finds a place to park up the street, and we exit the car. When Starsky spots the Feasters ahead, a low growl builds from inside. Andrew makes a *tsk* sound to get his attention. Then, with a touch of his hand on Starsky's head, the dog goes silent and watches with the rest of us. We've never taken any of our animals with us on a run, so I don't know what to expect, but with Andrew's new gift, the extra set of eyes will be helpful.

Following Emily's lead, we stop behind a tree. "Do you see her?" I ask.

The Feasters are blocking the way, so it's too difficult to assess. "I'm going to move across the street," Andrew whispers. "This way we can have multiple views."

"Don't do anything stupid," Emily begs. "Be careful." She moves toward him and plants a kiss on his cheek. Gathering her hand into his, he smiles. He doesn't need to say anything. Emily's free hand tucks wisps of hair behind her ear. "You really are a dork."

"No truer words have ever been said, but I'm your dork," he flirts, giving us a wink. He and Starsky cross the street. Once he's there, he waves his bat in the air. We move on either side of the street, trying to catch a glimpse of Carissa. As we approach, Feaster groans increase in volume. I'm guessing there are about a dozen of them. Based on the steady sound of their groaning, something's caught their attention. Then, as if on cue, we hear Carissa scream. We sneak behind the Feasters closest to us and one by one, we end them. Emily, with two hunting knives in her hands, sinks them into the backs of the skulls of two Feasters. Andrew trips up the Feaster closest to him, and in one motion brings his bat down onto its head. Then he spins around and ends the next two Feasters. *Ping! Ping!*

Carissa screams again. Emily holsters her knives and arms her bow with an arrow. We sprint towards the screams. When we arrive, she has her back against the iron gate where her house used to be. Five Feasters surround her. On the other side of the iron fencing, Case growls. Carissa, panic etched in her eyes, is using her staff to push them back as they approach. Emily sets her feet and drops two

Feasters with her bow and arrow. As I begin my approach towards Carissa, Emily stops me. "Wait!"

"Emily? We have to help her!"

"She's never going to be any good to us if we keep saving her. Let's see how she reacts."

"But," I say, trying to argue.

"No buts! Watch my back!" Then she turns and shouts, "Carissa! Remember what I taught you! Use your staff! Use your training!" Still panicked, she nods and lifts the staff over her head, ready to strike. She brings it down, splitting the skull of the Feaster in front of her. Then, as the Feaster to her left lunges forward, she brings the other side of the staff down, upending it. She uses the sharp end of the staff and plants it through the neck. Finally, she turns around, harnesses her staff, and makes a quick sprint towards the other, flipping over it and sticking the sharp end of the staff into the top of the Feaster's head. She lands, looking amazed at what she's done. Behind her, a Feaster sneaks. With a click of his tongue, Andrew looks down at Starsky, sending him racing towards the Feaster with Andrew close behind. Starsky barrels into the zombie, knocking him to the ground. Andrew comes in to finish the deal. *Ping!*

We have just a moment to catch our breath as we get to Carissa's side. Case, on the other side of the fence, reaches through the bars, hunger etched into his sunken eyes. "Well," Emily spits, "this is what you came here for, isn't it? Do it already so we can get out of here."

Carissa, shocked by Emily's aggressive tone, mutters, "How did you know I'd be here?"

"Are you kidding me? You're pretty easy to figure out. You told me you wanted to finish Case, so he didn't have to be out here. So, do it!"

Carissa's eyes well up with tears as a conflicted stare overtakes her face. I put my hand on Emily's shoulder and give it a light squeeze, hoping she takes it down a notch. Although this is a stupid move on Carissa's part, this can't be easy. I decide to chime in, "Carissa, I know this is hard, but you have to decide. We don't know how much time we have. There could be another herd heading this way. It's better if we are off the streets and back to safety."

She locks her brown eyes with mine. I nod, trying to relay the message everything will be okay. She nods back and wipes the tears from her eyes. "Okay, I'm going to do it." She readies her staff and points the sharp end towards Case. Her hands tremble like a leaf on a tree. A sound behind us interrupts the moment. Feasters? Yes, but there's something else. It's the sound of an engine. The four of us spin around and face the silhouettes of dozens upon dozens of approaching Feasters. Behind them is the dark outline of the van Emily and I followed to the warehouse. The growling and snapping of jaws fill our ears. Three larger Feasters lead the group and stop. To our disbelief, as if on command, the rest of the zombies behind them also stop. Andrew and I glance at each other. Could this be possible? Feasters that never do anything other than mindlessly search and feed on whatever is in their way, now following commands? It's as if the ones in front are controlling them. From behind us, we can hear Case growling, sensing the others are there.

The lights of the van turn on, carving beams of light past the Feasters. "What do we do, guys?" Andrew asks, nervousness bubbling just beneath the surface of his voice. "There are way too many of them."

Emily whispers in my ear, "We're going to need everything for this battle." I nod my head. "Even if we do, do you think we have a chance?"

"I don't know. We could make a run for it," I suggest.

"You know me, I'm always up for a fight," Emily spits, arming her bow.

Just then a voice, from what I presume is coming from some sort of speaker, shouts toward us, "We don't want any trouble!"

The four of us look at each other, astonished. "Well, you have a funny way of showing it. By the looks of things, it's all you want," I call out.

"I assure you that if we wanted trouble, we would already be upon you," the voice bellows. "We came for one thing."

"And what's that?" Andrew asks.

"Her!" the voice echoes, causing a frenzy from the Feasters as their groaning intensifies.

"Who? Me?" Emily shouts.

"Not you. The other her," the voice sounds amused, but humorless.

"Me?" Carissa whispers. "Why me? I don't even know these people."

We huddle up together, weighing our options, but the obvious choice is that there's no way we are letting Carissa go. "What do we do?" I ask.

"The way I look at it, we have two choices: fight our way out of this or make a run for it," Emily states.

"I don't know," Andrew mumbles, fear and wonder filling his words. "Did you see how those Feasters just stopped when those others did? This feels scary. Since when do they act like that or take commands?"

"Don't send me with them, please," Carissa pleads. "I've done everything I can do to be part of your family."

"Really? Like coming out here by yourself? What were you thinking?" Emily spits.

"Now's not the time, Emily," I remind her of our predicament.

"Okay, okay. I think we do both. See that house over there?" We follow where she's looking. "I bet if we fight our way to the house, we can make a break for the backyard, leap over the fence, and be on the next block. Once we're there, we should be safe. We keep moving until we get to Centre Square or hunker down in an abandoned house."

"What about the Camaro?" Andrew asks. Starsky whines at his side.

"We'll have to come back for it," Emily states. "I think it's our best way out."

The voice from the van booms, "So, what's it gonna be? My babies are getting hungry."

"Who is this guy?" Andrew asks. "Babies? If these are his babies, I'd hate to see what their mommy looks like."

"Let's have the girl, and everyone goes home," the guy in the van shouts. "You have my word."

"Your word? You're a grown man trying to scare a bunch of kids. Ever hear of stranger danger? We aren't letting her go with you," Emily spits.

"Tsk. Tsk. Have it your way." He whistles and the three at the front walk forward, and the Feasters behind them follow.

The four of us get in our fighting stance. "We stay tight together and drop anything that gets close," I instruct. "Emily, clear as many in the front as you can. Let's go."

Emily rears back an arrow and lets it fly toward the leader to the far right. He sees it coming and dodges out of the way. The arrow plants into the Feaster behind him. Emily drops the bow to her side in disbelief. She rears another arrow back, this time planting it into his leg. Although he stumbles, he still moves forward. Realizing she is going to have to act with precision and speed, she sends one arrow after another, dropping eight Feasters in all.

Emily shoulders her bow and arms herself with two knives. "I'm going to run out of arrows. We need to move." Before we can take another step, Emily screams. Something grabs Emily's wrist from behind. Looking down, she sees Case free from the yard, biting through her skin. She screams again from the pain and the shock of being bit. With one motion, she drives the hunting knife through the top of Case's skull, dropping him in a heap. Carissa gasps. We all look at Emily in disbelief. She looks down at her arm as blood pours from her wrist. "This isn't good," she spouts, attempting to grit through the pain.

"No, no, no, Emily, no!" I say, emotion overwhelming my body, which is stiff with fear. It's only a matter of time before she becomes one of them. And, when she does, I know I won't have the power to end her even though she'll tell me when the time comes. My heart sinks. We have to get her out of here. I won't let her walk with them. From behind us the Feasters are closing in, as the smell of fresh blood fills the air.

"How could I be so stupid?" she shouts. "I got caught up in what was in front of me –"

"That you didn't see what was behind you," I say, completing her thought.

Andrew drops to his knees, hands shaking, and attempts to bandage her arm. "There isn't time, you dummy. We've got to fight!"

"But what about your arm?" Andrew sniffles, choking back tears.

Emily lifts him from his knees. She kisses him on the lips. When she pulls away, she reminds him, "You know what this means. Don't let me turn out here. We have to go."

I look at the impossible task ahead of us. As the first Feasters get to us, I step out and hack away at them trying to will my body to transform, but it's not agreeing with me. Emily, with one good hand, does the best she can, but I can already tell by her complexion she doesn't look well. Carissa is frozen with fear. Emily sees this and shouts, "Hey! Remember your training!" Snapping out of it, she thrusts her staff into the throat of the first Feaster near her. With tears streaming from his eyes, Andrew swings wildly at anything in his way.

No matter how hard we fight, it's a losing battle. There are just too many of them. Looking off beyond the Feasters, the van creeps closer. I try to shout instructions, but the growling and groaning swallow my voice. Then Andrew does something unexpected. He steps back and lifts his arms up. From the trees lining the street, squawking, cawing and chirping rises to a deafening crescendo, shaking the leaves and branches. Then, he claps his hands echoing into the night air. All at once, every bird from trees and nearby foliage flock toward the herd. Their screams and chirps drown out the Feaster groans. The Feasters and their leaders turn their attention to the sky as the birds swarm in like a feathery tornado. They dive and peck at them, poking holes in decaying flesh.

Seeing the distracted Feasters, Andrew shouts, "Now's our chance! Let's go!" I grab Emily's arm and put it over my shoulder and the four of us and Starsky bolt through the hoard of Feasters, dodging, weaving, and taking down some of the distracted ones.

When we get to the Camaro, Emily attempts to get into the driver's seat. "It's my turn." I take the keys from her hand. It concerns me that she doesn't put up a fight. Instead, she piles into the back with Andrew and Starsky. I turn the key and the Camaro roars. Unsure of how to drive, I let instinct take over. Knowing we need to make a quick U-turn, I shift it into drive and cut the wheel hard to the left while flooring the gas pedal. The Camaro's rear tires roar and spin wildly as the front of the car pitches left. The car's torque turns the car around, and we fishtail down the street and away from the van and the herd of Feasters.

My concern shifts to Emily. I know we don't have long before she turns. I'm not sure what getting her back to Sebastian Labs would do. We agreed a long time ago that if either of us was to get bitten, we would end it for the other when we turn. "How's she doing, Andrew?"

"Why are you asking him?" Emily mumbles, her voice weak. She coughs. "I'm still here."

"Well, how are you feeling?" I ask.

"I've always wondered what it would feel like when the change happens. I'm feeling weak, but I can actually feel my blood changing in my veins. I can't explain it. It's warming my body."

"Hang in there!" I look in the rearview mirror as I race through the streets. Andrew's face shows his pain. It's emotional and swollen, as if he's been crying for hours.

"Andrew," Emily says.

"Save your strength, Em," Andrew pleads.

"There's no time for that, listen to me. My life has felt so complete with you. I dreamed we would get older, get married, and start a family." She pauses a second, overwhelmed with tears. "I'm so happy I got the tingles that day."

"Yeah," Andrew sniffles and tries to laugh. "You almost drove an arrow into me."

"Well, yeah, there's that. But I'm glad I didn't. I'm happy I turned you. Andrew, I love you." They embrace each other. Andrew whispers his love for her in her ear.

Seeing this hollows out my soul, and my heart breaks. "And you, Kieran. I couldn't have asked for a better partner in the apocalypse," she laughs without energy, choking back tears. She coughs and struggles to catch her breath. "You have always been so strong for us. Your mother and father would be so proud of your leadership, companionship, and love for Andrew and me. I have always loved that you're my cousin."

There's no way to control my emotions. My body shakes. I try to be strong. "I love that *you're* my cousin. We're going to get you back to Sebastian Labs. Get you comfortable."

Only the roar of the engine fills the space. "Kieran, don't take me back there. I've changed my mind. Let me off somewhere. You know what's happening to me. I'm turning. It won't be safe. Stop the car and let me out."

Andrew protests, "Emily, that's not going to happen."

"You know it's the right thing to do."

"We'll cross that bridge when we get to it. Let's just get you there."

Emily is too weak to argue. Instead, she passes out in Andrew's arms.

"No, no, no, Emily. Stay with me. C'mon, stay with me," Andrew pleads, tears spilling down the corners of his eyes. Then to me he pleads, "Kieran, she's so warm. She's burning up."

"Andrew," I whisper with urgency in my voice. "Don't let your guard down. She can turn at any moment." Andrew continues to embrace her, running his fingers through her long, red hair. "Andrew, you must listen! We don't know when she'll turn."

With frustration and anger in his voice, he bites back, "I heard you, Kieran! I've got this!" After he gathers himself, he asks, "What can we do? We can't lose her."

"This is all my fault. I can't do anything right. This is all my fault. Kieran, I'm sorry," Carissa sobs, forcing herself to look over at Emily.

It's true. This is all her fault, but right now our focus must be on Emily. For the first time in a long time, I don't know what to do. Like a bad dream I can't wake up from, I shudder at the idea of living without Emily. My head swims. My hands tremble. Wild thoughts race around my brain like an untamed stallion. I wish this was one of my dreams because I always wake up from them, but this... this is one I can't escape. I long to talk to my mother right now. She'd know what to do. Wait... my dream. When I went snooping, I found that file about the cure. It's a long shot, but could the cure help Emily? "Carissa. Look at me. The cure. What do you know about the cure? About the process. Does your father have any more of the cure at Sebastian Labs?"

"Yes. That, I know for sure. It's stored in an office down at the end of the hallway. I've seen my father use it a few times. I'm not sure if I can," she chokes through tears.

"What do you think if we hook up Emily to the cure, would you know what to do?"

"But, when we tried it on my mother, it failed," Carissa reminds us.

"Yes, but this time we'll have –"

"Pure Vampire blood!" Carissa states, a twinge of excitement in her voice.

Looking in the rearview mirror, I make sure no one is following us. I frantically squeeze the gas pedal of the Camaro and roar past the last few blocks to Sebastian Labs.

Chapter 9

Fix Her

When we arrive at Sebastian Labs, I don't worry about parking a few blocks away the way Emily prefers because she doesn't want to draw attention to Sebastian Labs. I bring the Camaro to a screeching, skidding halt just inches from the wall. I rush out of the car and help Andrew carry Emily. She's not responsive, her body's temperature is an inferno, and her skin is losing its porcelain color. As we rush to the door, Carissa is still in the passenger seat with a blank stare on her face. I shout, "Carissa! Hey, let's go!"

"I don't know if I can do this," she cries.

"Look, we don't have time for any insecurities. Emily is going to die and turn into one of them if we don't do something soon! Get out of the car and lead us to the lab. While we're on our way, you are going to need to do your best to remember everything you can about the cure. Everything. We don't have time," I demand from Carissa. Seeing the pain and confusion on her face, I finish by saying, "Carissa. You can do this. I mean, we believe in you." Andrew nods.

"Okay. Okay," she resolves, understanding we need her to step up. Getting out of the car, she shakes her hands as if they just received a jolt of electricity and gathers her nerves. She sprints to the back, inserts the key into the lock, and unlatches the door. She leads the way through hallways.

Andrew and I flank Emily on either side, one arm under each leg and the other behind her back and follow. Carissa leads down the stairs to the hallway where our sleeping quarters are. She bolts ahead of us to the laboratory. Rushing in, she demands, "Put her on that gurney!" Andrew and I do as we're told. "Make sure you strap her arms down," she demands. Strap her arms? Is she crazy? Carissa senses us staring at her with confused looks on our faces. "What are you guys doing? Strap her arms down."

"Really? Do we have to strap her down?" Andrew asks, confused. "It's Emily. C'mon."

Then, we see a side of Carissa we haven't seen before. "I know it's Emily. It doesn't erase the fact that she's bitten." This doesn't force us to act. "Look! Emily's bit. She's infected. Since she's infected, she can turn." The last words she declares slowly and deliberately, like a parent on the edge of scolding a child, "If what we are going to do goes horribly wrong, we need to make sure we take all precautions. Given how close you are to Emily, your reaction may not be as quick as it usually is. Right?" Our blank stares give her the answer. "Now, do what I asked you to do. Strap her hands down, please."

The both of us shake our heads in agreement and move to strap Emily down. I look up to see Carissa walking out of the room and say, "Hey, where ya going?"

"I'm getting my father's work. The cure. In the meantime, open that cabinet behind you and pull out anything that looks important. Needles, syringes, tape, gauze. If you think it will help, grab it. Andrew, in the room there." Carissa points to what looks like a closet. "There's an IV pole." She sees the confused look on his face. "An intravenous pole. It holds bags of fluid and stuff like that. I'll be right back." She rushes out of the room.

Andrew and I do what she asks of us and try our best to have everything ready for when she returns. Once I have everything on the metallic tray next to the gurney, I turn to look at Emily. She looks terrible. Without doubt, the Feaster cells are multiplying. Her eyes retreat into her skull, surrounded by greying darkness where her fair skin once welcomed smiling green eyes. My heart feels crushed. If we lose... if I lose Emily, I'm not sure I would have enough strength to move on and survive. I run my fingers through her hair and notice her fiery red hair color now looks muted; its luster fading. I lean down to whisper to her. To tell her it's all going to be okay. As I move close to her ear, her body radiates with such heat, I'm surprised and pause for a moment thinking about when Harold leaned down to Marisol, and she bit him. Still, I move closer. Andrew's hand rests on my back and I can hear him sniffling. "Emily," I whisper. Her head moves ever so slightly in my direction. "Emily." My body trembles, searching for the right words to say. "I know you're in there. We need you to fight. If anyone can fight off those hideous Feaster cells, it's you. You have your bow already loaded picking off those nasty things," I laugh, fighting off waves of emotion swelling inside. "I don't think I can do this without you. I don't *want* to do this without you." My eyes pour streams of tears.

I look up and meet Andrew's eyes. His emotions match mine. I walk around to the other side of the gurney and hug him, giving him permission to heave waves of tears into my shoulder. I pull away and look at him. Nodding my head, I say, "We gotta believe there's still a chance. It's all we have."

"I know. I know."

Carissa barges into the room carrying two IV bags and some other supplies while rolling in some kind of machine. "Okay, here we go. I think I've got everything we need. Andrew, have you ever given someone a needle or a shot?"

"Just a shot. My little brother had diabetes, so I helped him with shots before."

"That's a start. Since we are running short on time, I need you to start an IV on Emily's arm."

"What? I don't know how to do that!" Andrew stammers.

"Look at me. It's easy. Not exactly the same as a shot, but at least you will be comfortable with a needle." She hands the needle to him. "Find a good vein in Emily's forearm. You are going to insert the needle into the vein. Pull back on this plunger a little until it fills with some blood. Then, you are golden. Gently pull out the needle but leave the catheter in there."

"The what?" Andrew asks, panicked.

"The catheter," she says as she begins mixing the solution and priming the tubing. "It's a little rubber tube which stays in the vein. It's the only way the medicine can get into her system. Once the needle is out, take this tape and fasten the catheter into place." Andrew, his hands shaking, takes the supplies. "Andrew. This is the simple part. You can do this."

As Andrew sets to work on Emily, Carissa turns to me, "You. Take off your coat, roll up your sleeve, and get on this gurney." She pats the gurney next to Emily.

She sets to getting the needle into my arm. I've always hated needles, but I'm surprised when I look down and Carissa already has it in there with only a pinch. "You're good at this. I knew you would step up when we needed you to."

"Yeah, well, it's the least I can do. I'm the reason Emily is in this mess," Carissa tears up.

"There's no time for insecurity. Let's go, you've got this!" I lay down.

"I did it!" Andrew shouts from the other gurney.

"Good job. Now I need you to hang both bags on this IV stand and roll it next to Emily's head."

Andrew sets to work while Carissa connects the tubing from my arm to the machine. "What's that thing?" I ask, recognizing it when Harold had Andrew hooked up to it when he tried to cure Marisol.

"This here is a pump. This is what's going to take your blood and deliver it to Emily." As she is connecting the tubing, she continues, "The bag with the greyish fluid in there? This is the formula, the cure. I mixed it with the saline in the IV bag. My father explained that when combined with your blood – pure Vampire blood – it's supposed to do two things: strengthen the cells that are fighting off the Feaster cells and restore those Feaster cells into something else, returning them to near normal.

"What else?" I ask.

"I don't know. Most of the stuff my father told me was way over my head. The entire process is going to be taxing on her body. The saline will keep her hydrated." Carissa moves the tubing through the opening in the pump and runs it into what looks like an intersection which goes into Emily's arm. The other part of the tubing goes up into another intersection, which splits up into the bag with the cure and the other into the saline solution. After connecting the primed tubing to the IV in Emily's arm, she asks, "Alright? Ready to go?"

I nod my head. "How long will this take?"

"I'm not sure. Father never used more than one bag of the cure. But, as far as results go, I don't know. It's never been successful. I guess we have to wait and see."

"Okay, then let's get started," I say, feeling my voice tremble.

Carissa moves over to the pump and turns it on. Blood crawls from my body through the tubing and into Emily. Andrew grabs a chair and sits next to Emily and engulfs her hand and kisses it. He looks at me with swollen eyes, concern chiseled in them. I try to shoot him a confident wink, but it feels forced, and I know Andrew sees right through it.

Taking inventory of my emotions, I can say this is the most scared I've ever been. Facing down a herd of Feasters easily dulls compared to the prospect of losing Emily. To watch her slow, painful transition to becoming a zombie is far worse. The other time I'd been this fearful and not in control of things was when Harold nearly killed Andrew. We'd thought we lost him that day. My mind races to my parents. I wonder if this is the level of fear my father felt the day my mother was brought to the hospital. The horror of watching life being drained from someone must be hard, but from a loved one, it's a burden no one should ever have to go through. Now I find myself having to experience this twice with two of the most important people in my life.

Looking over at Emily, I notice her complexion doesn't get better. Her skin yellows and the flesh surrounding her eyes is dark grey, like an ominous sky promising storms and destruction. Lifting my head, I notice I feel weak and lightheaded. "Carissa, is it working?" I ask.

She has a concerned look on her face bordering on fear or doubt. "Kieran, I don't know. I think it may be too soon, but truthfully, I'm not sure. There's only a little left of the cure in the bag. So, we should see results soon. I just don't know when."

"Why do I feel so weak?" I ask.

"It's because of the blood you are giving to Emily. It's quite a bit. Only a little while longer, I promise. Hang in there," she tries to reassure me and moves some hair out of my eyes.

"Umm, Carissa? Something is wrong!" Andrew yells.

With little strength left, I look at Emily. Her eyes, which had a half appearance of a Feaster, were open but started rolling up into her head. From her mouth, foam bubbles up and spills out of the sides. Like getting electrocuted, her arms and legs shake. Suddenly, her chest lifts while her head pitches back. A gurgling sound echoes in the silent room. Then, Emily lets out a primal scream so loud the room shakes, "Noooooooooooooo!" Her chest heaves several times before her secured arms flail like a rabid dog trying to free itself from its collar and chains. Her legs kick wildly, narrowly missing Andrew several times. I can't bear to watch Emily's face as it tenses and blood seeps and mixes with the foam still bubbling from her mouth.

Andrew tries to calm Emily as best he could, but it's no use. Carissa darts over to Emily's side, turns off the pump, and shouts, "Andrew, there's nothing you can do! She's having a seizure!"

"Why is this happening? What did you do to her?" Andrew screams, his eyes begin to glow. Starsky, sensing Andrew's discomfort, barks wildly at the unfolding events.

"I don't know why it's happening!"

"Well, fix it, Carissa!" Andrew growls.

From behind them, I feel my body grow weaker. With a whimper, I cry out to Emily.

Carissa, now on her way to sobbing, defends herself, "I don't know how to fix it! I don't know what to do!"

"Fix her! Fix Emily!" Andrew's fangs drop and his eyes rage brighter.

Carissa, with a look of panic, fear, and anger, screams, "I CAN'T!"

As I lose consciousness from the blood loss, I watch Emily's body arch once more and then drop flat on the gurney and become still. My eyes grow heavier with each passing second. Andrew's body drapes over Emily's. My eyes close and open again. Carissa turns to look at me, astonishment and disbelief plastered across her face. She grabs fistfuls of her own hair, covers her ears, and screams. Her body drops to the floor in a heap. No matter how hard I try to keep them open, my eyes close again.

Chapter 10

A Death in the Family

"Kieran? Wake up. Can you hear me?" Emily's soft voice wakes me. "C'mon sleepyhead. You've been asleep for hours."

My vision is a haze as I blink, trying to clear it. A blurry outline of Emily stands over me. "Emily? Is that really you?" She comes into focus. "I – I thought you were dead. I saw you on the gurney. You made it? Oh, thank God," I say, struggling to find my voice.

"Of course I made it. I'm Emily Estrie," her voice echoes with laughter.

"But… but... never mind. I'm so happy to see you." Her skin returns to its normal porcelain complexion and her hair is a vibrant red. I look around the room, searching for Andrew and Carissa. Something doesn't feel right. This room feels familiar. We aren't in Sebastian Labs; we're in Emily's bedroom. "Why are we here?" I ask.

Emily cocks her head slightly to the side. "Here?"

"Yes, your room."

She shakes her head, not understanding my confusion. "Kieran, we've never left."

Bolting up to a seating position, I scan the room searching again. "Emily, where are Andrew and Carissa?"

"It's a bit of a long story. Let's just say they didn't make it," she vocalizes with a flippant pep in her voice.

I'm so confused as I swing my feet off the edge of a bed. "Emily, look at me. That's not much of a story at all."

She laughs, "I guess you're right."

"So, what happened?" My eyes burn into hers, begging for answers.

"Well, where to begin? You see, they wanted her."

"Who? Carissa?" My eyes widen as the realization hits me. "Who wants her?"

"The Circle. They want her. It's what the revenge game is all about."

What the heck is she talking about? The Circle? Revenge game? Why does The Circle sound so familiar? "Em. What is The Circle?"

"You already know. It'll come to you." She stares at me, pursing her lips, raising her eyebrows as if waiting for the revelation to come. It doesn't.

"Okay, so what happened to them!?"

"There was nothing I could do. We're one of them. We can't betray our own."

"They took her?"

"Yes," Emily announces, shrugging her shoulders. "She was a burden for us. It's much, much better this way," Emily says, crossing her arms in front of her and throwing them to her side like she's discarding something. Something meaningless.

"What are you talking about? How could you let that happen?" More of a question of disbelief. "So, what happened to Andrew?"

She rolls her eyes, "You know Andrew. He didn't see things the same as The Circle, and they didn't like it."

"Emily, where is he?"

"They took him too. I'm going to miss him. He was really cute."

"Gonna miss him? You say that like you're giving up drinking pig's blood. Don't you care about him?"

"Well, yeah, but... you know. It wasn't going to work. It's the apocalypse for Pete's sake."

This isn't the Emily I know. I don't understand what's happening. Just then, sounds of Feasters come from the stairs leading up to her room. Emily hears this and moves toward the door. "What are you doing?"

"They're calling for me. I have to go," Emily says, her head cocked as if I should know the answer.

I dart to the door to stand in her way. "What's wrong with you? You don't even have a weapon."

"Kieran, you're being strange," she snickers. "There's no danger outside this door. They are waiting for me. I have to go." She takes hold of both my shoulders, easily guides me out of the way, and opens the door.

"Emily, no. Don't go out there! You can't be serious!"

"Of course, I am. I can't keep them or your mother waiting," she chuckles and heads out of the room.

My mother? I peer down the stairs, looking for her, but Feasters crowd the stairwell, and like when I dreamt of my mother, the Feasters move out of the way for Emily the same way they did for her. I know it's not real because Emily would have hacked through the entire herd. So, I know this is a dream, but what does it mean? It's rare that I realize I'm dreaming. As Emily reaches the bottom of the stairs, I see her. Mother waits for her and allows Emily to pass. She looks up at me, smiles, and her voice echoes, "He's not dead." She turns to walk out of the door and like before, the Feasters follow her.

I awaken from my dream with my mother's words echoing, *He's not dead. He's not dead.* It's then Emily races to my mind. The bite. The cure. The seizure. My eyes bolt back and forth, running the events over and over in my mind before I passed out. I passed out! How long have I been out?

My body jolts to a sitting position. I find myself in bed in our sleeping quarters in Sebastian Labs. Where is everyone? Where's Emily? Is she okay?

I move into the hallway, and everything is quiet. The sole sign of life comes from the dim, flickering light from the laboratory where we tried the cure on Emily. Sprinting down the hall, I wonder where Andrew and Carissa are. When I get to the laboratory, my entire world changes. Through the window, I see the empty gurney where I laid. On the other gurney, a white sheet covers what appears to be a body. Sitting on the ground, next to the gurney, is an exhausted Andrew. His head rests back against the gurney; his eyes sunken in and bloodshot. Starsky rests across his lap.

I creep into the room, approaching Andrew. "Hey," I choke out a whisper.

Andrew looks at me as if he's seeing a ghost. "Kieran?"

"Is that –," I say, but I can't commit to saying her name. To say her name means that what happened is real.

Before I can, Andrew springs to his feet and buries his face into my shoulder. In between shuddered breaths, he spouts, "We tried, Kieran. We tried!"

"What?!" I ask, fearing the worst. "What?!"

"Emily, Kieran. It's Emily. She's... she's dead." Andrew buries himself into my shoulder again as if saying it out loud released another round of raw emotion.

The room spins. My eyes flutter, searching for something to keep anchored upon. Emily. My eyes focus on Emily's body resting under the sheet. I peel myself from Andrew's embrace and approach her. I'm afraid to remove the sheet – to know this is real. Taking a deep breath, I pull it back. She looks so peaceful, like she's asleep, as if she's going to jump up and reveal how she tricked me. For moments, I wait. For moments, I pray she tries to scare me. But she doesn't. She just lays there. Her hair lacks the vibrance it once had and lays limp, fanned out across her shoulder and hangs off the gurney. I look over at her face. She looks like a doll waiting for someone to play with. The kind when someone stands them upright, their eyes open. I want to pick her up. Hold her in my arms. See her eyes open. Instead, I feel my body become heavy. Grief takes over and pulls me down across her. I accept the fact that Emily's dead. And with this realization, emotion overcomes my body and I release. I release tears. I release anger. I release a scream. "Nooooooo!" I feel Andrew's hand on my back. We stay like this, frozen in time as if trapped in a photograph, trapped in a nightmare.

When my mind can no longer give any more to the moment, I stand up and face Andrew. Our faces match each other in emotion and distress, caped in loss. "How long was I out for?"

"Nearly two days."

"Have you been with her the entire time?"

"Most of it except to check on you," Andrew manages a half-smile.

"What the heck happened?"

Andrew's eyes search the room, trying to piece together the events. "How much do you remember?"

"I remember being hooked up to the IV and Carissa trying to give Emily the cure. Speaking of Carissa, where is she?"

"Once we realized that Emily…" Andrew chokes out the words, "was dead, she ran into her room, and I haven't seen her since."

Shifting my thoughts to Emily, I say, "So, tell me what happened."

Andrew sits on the floor beside the gurney where Emily rests and gathers his thoughts. "Everything was going fine. Not fine that the cure was working or anything like that. Fine, as in everything was going as planned, I guess. Then she started shaking. The next thing we know, Emily burst into a full-blown seizure."

"Yeah, I remember that. Foam and blood spilled from her mouth. And her body jerked all over the place and then… and then she went limp."

"Yup, after she did, I looked over and you were out."

"So, what happened next?" I ask.

"It was a nightmare. After the both of you became quiet, Carissa and I looked over Emily's body. Checking for vitals, heartbeat and breathing. Stuff like that. Kieran, she didn't have a pulse."

"That's it?"

"No. We were staring at each other in complete disbelief, not knowing what to do next. An audible intake of air ripped into the silence, like someone gasping after holding their breath for too long. When we looked down, Emily glared right at Carissa. With her hand still strapped down, she grabbed Carissa's hand and growled, 'YOU! YOU! YOU!' Then, she gasped again as if trying to hold on. As quick as it started, it ended, and her body became limp."

I stand, shaking my head in disbelief. "That must have been terrible," I admit, trying to picture the events.

"Kieran, that wasn't even the worst part. I'll never forget what her face looked like."

"Her face?"

"Yes. Her teeth extended and still had saliva and blood all over them. But her eyes. Her eyes sent shivers down my spine. Hazed over like Feaster eyes, as if she had fully transformed. But, behind them, they were red. Not just red, but like a light glowing through a fog, except it was brighter and clearer. Like when she gets mad and her instincts kick in, but brighter. Radiating. It made me squint. Almost as if her Vampire side was becoming one with a Feaster."

"What? C'mon, seriously?"

"I'm being serious, Kieran. Like a bad punchline to a joke. What do you get when you cross a zombie and Vampire? But... but the answer is something you can't describe. You don't want to describe. You know things rarely get me frazzled, but this... this freaked me out."

I notice Andrew's eyes, a mixture of pain, sadness, and disbelief. I put my hand on his shoulder and give it a quick squeeze. "Andrew, I'm sorry you had to go through this alone. I can't imagine seeing Emily like that. I'm pretty sure I never want to either." We look over at her body. My mind is still having trouble accepting any of this is real. "I guess the one thing I can be thankful for is she never had to change into one of those things."

"Or we didn't have to face her like that or do what we do to Feasters," Andrew utters, unable to say the word 'kill'.

"I don't know if either of us would have the strength to do it," I admit. Andrew acknowledges by nodding his head in agreement, choking back another onset of emotion.

"So, what do we do with her? Should we have a service? A burial? What's the Vampire thing to do?"

It's not something I want to think about, but I know it has to be done. "Tomorrow's the third day. When a Vampire dies, we wait until the third day to bury them. Tomorrow's perfect, I guess."

"Where are we gonna do it? Was there a place special to her?"

It hits me, "I think I know. You know the enormous cedar tree in Centre Square?" Andrew nods. "Our family used to spend a lot of time there, especially when the town put on events. We'd always get there early because Emily insisted it's where the most fireflies were."

"Fireflies?"

"Anytime she was near them, they surrounded her as if they wanted to be near her. It didn't matter who was around, they always followed her like snow flurries in a storm. And... and they would land on her too. No one else, just her. It was like... like…" I struggle to find the words as emotion overcomes me.

"Like magic?" Andrew finishes my sentence.

"Yes," I smile, thinking how much the fireflies made her happy. "She always had control of the things around her." I nod my head. "That's where we're going to lay her to rest. She'd approve."

Andrew's eyes are now glassy pools. "Perfect."

"Tomorrow then," I say, satisfied with the decision. "Let's get some sleep." I sense some hesitation in Andrew. "What's up?"

"What about Em?"

I look over her body, dreading tomorrow, knowing I will never hear her goofy laugh or listen to one of her sarcastic jokes. Most of all, I will miss my cousin, my partner in crime for my entire life, and my friend. I want to walk over to her and shake her awake. I want this to be a poor joke, but I know it's not. "She'll be here in the morning. She'd want us to take care of ourselves."

I clap Andrew on the back and walk over to Emily. He follows. We both give her a kiss on her forehead and gently cover her with the sheet. We look at each other and embrace in a hug. Devastation was destined to find us, no matter how hard we fought it. It doesn't mean were prepared for it.

As we walk out of the room, Andrew asks, "What are we going to do about Carissa?"

I peer down the hallway and see Carissa's door. With all that's happened, I realize I hadn't thought much about her. A flood of ick settles into my thoughts. Ick about the situation. Ick about Carissa's carelessness. Just ick. I'd spent so much time trying to defend her to Emily. I didn't want to believe she's a liability. I'm not fully sold on that idea. But I also didn't listen to Emily's concerns and frustration with her. She knew. She always knew. Even way back to that fateful night when Carissa shined the stupid flashlight in the window, she knew. That's why she pushed Carissa so hard during training. She didn't get revenge by humiliating her, but knowing Emily, she enjoyed the idea. However, Emily wanted to protect us by making Carissa less of a liability. So, at this moment, I'm not sure what to think about Carissa. What I know is she needs to understand her position with us and how dangerous stupid decisions can be. I'm angry. I've tried not to blame her for all of this, but I know this. She is responsible for Emily's death, and I'm not sure her offense is forgivable.

Chapter 11

That Wasn't a Feaster

Given the circumstances, I'm surprised that sleep welcomes me, but it isn't deep. While I struggle to get there, I will myself to dream. Although my dreams are uncomfortable and often unpleasant, they sometimes offer some kind of clarity or control. Now, more than ever, I *need* that clarity and control. Something to help make sense of what is happening. Maybe clarity isn't what I'll get. Perhaps there aren't any signs. Perhaps Emily's death is just that – a death, and there's no warning or meaning to any of it. I wonder why Emily didn't change into a Feaster. The cure must have something to do with it. So, no dream comes. Instead, sleep finds me, but I can't tell how long it is before I am woken up by Starsky's whining.

I rub the sleep from my eyes and see Andrew's already at Starsky's side. He's kneeling down on one knee, whispering, "What is it, boy?" He licks Andrew's face once and focuses on the door again.

Finding my voice, I whisper, "What's happening?"

"Starsky senses something is out in the hallway," Andrew chokes out. He looks concerned, as if sensing what Starsky is feeling.

"It's probably just Carissa," I say.

"It could be, but…" A loud POP and the shattering of glass interrupt Andrew's words. We freeze in our tracks, eyes wide with fear and anticipation. We hear the desperate squeal of one pig. It's quick and then it's silent. "What the heck is happening?" He sees me reach for my machete, and it cues him to find his bat. Starsky, a little unnerved by the sound, cowers behind Andrew's legs. Without warning, a guttural scream fills the hallway outside of our room, making the walls shake. Feaster? Sounds like it, but this is more forceful than we've ever heard from a Feaster before.

I decide we have to act. Reaching for the door, I open it as if whatever is in the hallway is right outside. Andrew and Starsky follow. Nothing could prepare us for what we see. Glass from the containment room, where the pigs live, lay like pieces of ice throughout the hallway. That isn't what frightens us. The remains of Big Bertha lay scattered in bloody heaps. Something's torn into her and feasted on her insides. The smell of pig's blood fills my senses and fires my Vampire instincts. Although I'm scared, the need to feed confuses my mind.

"Zombies?" Andrew asks, choking out like he's chewing gravel.

"It would seem like it, but how? And where did they go?" Then, as if on cue, a massive, shadowy figure down the hallway catches my eye. "There!" I point. Andrew sees it and we ready our weapons.

The figure squares off against us and then in a flash, it moves with a blur across the hall and through the exit door to the stairs, slamming it shut. "Um, have you ever seen a Feaster move that fast?" Andrew wonders.

"That wasn't a Feaster."

"Duh, ya think?"

Carissa's door opens, and she peeks out. She whispers in a hurried breath, "What was that noise?"

Andrew replies with urgency cemented into his words, "Carissa, close the door and lock it. Don't come out until we get you."

"Why?"

Andrew snaps, "Just do it. We'll explain later."

Andrew, Starsky, and I race down the hallway, weaving around the decimated pig and reaching the door. With fear pulsing through our veins, we open it and see a trail of blood up the stairs. Keeping our eyes peeled we follow the trail. We track it up to the main floor. The metal of the doorknob, covered with blood, is squished like a foil pan. I look back at Andrew, confusion etched across my face. "Feasters that can open doors?"

"Whoa, what is that?" Claw marks appear on the edge of the door, traced into the metal frame like an etching on a plaque.

"Kieran, this is definitely no Feaster. I don't know what this is, but I'm pretty freaked out."

"Yeah, me too. Be ready," I say, dropping my fangs as my eyes glow. Andrew does the same. Starsky looks ready too, determined to follow the trail. I open the door and it occurs to me I have no concept of time. The blast of sunshine rips into the hallway and knocks Andrew and me off our feet. Its heat and light searing into our exposed flesh; hands and faces. Andrew swipes at the door with his foot, closing it. We lay there gasping for air and longing for the pain to cease.

As we are struggling to recover, Carissa's voice cuts in, "Boys? Something's wrong."

Carissa steps back when I spin around to see her, my body mid-transformation into its full Vampire potential and my burned skin healing. "Yes," I growl. "It's obvious something is wrong. What gave you that idea? Is it the fact we are on the floor in pain?"

Andrew chimes in, his body still unable to reach full potential. "I thought we told you to stay in your room."

She gathers herself and squares her shoulders. "I'm not something you can tell what to do and how to do it. Now listen to me and shut up for a second. Yes, there's something wrong here. I'm not an idiot. But, there's something else." Panic starts its way into her voice as the enormity of the situation hits like a flood all at once. "It's Emily."

"What about her?" I ask, the gruff leaving my voice as my body returns back to normal.

"She's – she's gone."

Andrew and I shoot confused glances at each other. He asks, "What do you mean *gone*? Do you mean like 'passed away'? Yes, we already knew that. So did you." Andrew throws his hands in the air in frustration.

"No, I mean gone as in like not here. Like poof. Gone!" Carissa yells.

I turn to run back downstairs to the laboratory room where Emily's body rests. By the time I gather the courage to open the door, Andrew and Carissa are behind me. Pushing open the door, I can see Carissa is right, Emily is gone. Her gurney rests on its side as if a struggle happened. Bodily fluid, of what I perceive by the smell to be vomit, mixed with blood, pools on the floor and spills towards the drain in the middle of the room. Droplets create a trail towards the door where we stand. I look around the room, trying to find other clues.

Andrew and Starsky barge past me. Starsky rushes up to the puddle to inspect. Andrew clicks his tongue and Starsky stops in his tracks and returns to Andrew's side. "What happened here? Where's Emily?"

We stare at each struggling to make sense of things. "Did that Feaster or whatever the heck that thing was..." I say, struggling to get the next words out.

"Eat her?" Andrew finishes my thoughts, and his body quivers at the thought.

I spin around the room, looking for any signs of Emily. "No, that can't be it. When have we ever known a Feaster to eat everything and not leave any evidence? Other than the muck on the floor, there's no sign of anything else that even shows it attacked her. And whatever that thing was down the hallway wasn't carrying anything when it left."

"Then where is she, Kieran?"

"I don't know, but I'm freaking out a little. Nothing makes sense," I admit, shaking my head.

"I think I can make sense of what happened." Carissa's voice comes from the doorway, her face blanketed with awe and bewilderment.

Chapter 12

History of the Cure

"What do you mean you can make sense of this?" I shoot a look as sharp as a dagger at Carissa. Around every turn there's another secret hiding in the shadows of the Croger family. From the time Carissa and Harold lured us to the house, to trying to freeze Marisol's transformation and reverse the Feaster process, to hiding Case in a cage, or the cure itself, there's always something which builds my disdain towards this family. I remind myself Carissa isn't to blame, but around every one of these turns, it feels like she knows more than she lets on. And now, she knows what happened to Emily, just like how she knew about administering the cure. "You need to get to talking, now!"

"You see, well…" Carissa struggles on where to start.

"Start talking! What happened to Emily?" Andrew grits out. Starsky whines.

"I'm trying. I don't know where to begin."

"How about starting with where Emily is," I say, softening my stance, realizing our heightened frustration may make it hard for her to explain.

"Okay, long story short: I believe a Feaster didn't take Emily away, nor did another creature. Whatever made those noises, the destruction of the hallway and window, and the death of our poor pig *is* our Emily."

Andrew and I stare at Carissa as she waits for us to catch up with her thinking. Finally, Andrew speaks, "That's impossible! She's dead, Carissa! What's your angle here?"

"Yes, she's dead, but she may also be alive."

"That's ridiculous," I scoff. "You can't be both things."

"I agree. We can't. But *she* can," Carissa observes, marveling at her own words.

"You're telling us that the thing in the hallway *was* Emily? It was double our size, and it tore through Bertha like a piñata," Andrew cries.

"Okay, enough is enough. What are you talking about? I bet this has something to do with the cure."

"Yes. The vomit all over the floor was the first clue. As my father grew more and more desperate to save my mother and brother and make right the mess he made, he made more and more tweaks to the formula. Before Mother was bitten, we would spend some time here at Sebastian Labs. He and a few of the scientists who didn't turn or run away worked day and night on the cure. When they brought in test subjects –"

"Test subjects? Just call them what they were. Prisoners. Victims. Take your pick," I insist.

"Call them what you like. But my father wanted me to watch the experiments, so I learned how to do them. I'm guessing just in case he didn't make it or something else. He was always talking about science with me. That's how I knew how to try the cure on Emily."

"A lot of good that did her."

Carissa half rolls her eyes, ignoring my statement. "Originally, my father's work focused on curing Vampirism." Carissa waits, expecting a reaction. I say nothing, but frustration simmers under the surface. "Things went bad in the lab that day. When the zombies came to life, of course, he shifted his focus on fixing his miscalculation." I struggle to contain a sarcastic chuckle. "So, most of the subjects brought in were regular zombies. You know, humans bitten and turned. Every one of them failed. When he tweaked the formula, he got some results. Nothing over the top. A heartbeat or two. Some complexion changes. Promising, but nothing that was going to end the apocalypse."

"Okay, we get it," Andrew conveys, "but what does this have to do with Emily?"

"It wasn't until he got some subjects who were originally Vampires where things started to change. He told me since Vampire blood differs from human blood, he wondered if the cure would be effective in changing zombies back to Vampires. He felt that would at the very least be progress."

"So, what happened?" I ask, captivated in the story.

"Nothing."

"Nothing? What the heck? I feel like we are running out of time, and we aren't one step closer to knowing what happened!" I feel my patience waning.

"Well, not exactly nothing," Carissa rolls her eyes. "They didn't turn back to Vampires, but when he looked at their blood, he noticed the cure did something to the blood cells. I never understood all he was trying to say, but I knew it had to be something important. So, he changed the cure and then something happened. One day, they brought in a zombie who used to be a Vampire. My father tried the new cure on her and just like what happened to Emily, it didn't work... at first. Then, she started showing signs of change. Heart rate. Coloring. A few days later, she sat up."

"Did it work?" Andrew asks, wide eyes revealing his wonder.

"Well, not exactly. Not long after, she grew sick and vomited as if someone had turned on a garden hose, but instead of fresh water, the worst smelling gunk poured out. Then, she died. My father knew he was close. He obsessed day and night over it. Finally, one day, he had a breakthrough. He infused the cure with Vampire blood. The zombie showed the same signs of recovery."

"Including the throwing up part?" I ask.

"Even that."

"Then what happened?"

"We don't know. Just like Emily, a few days later, he took off. He broke through the glass window and out into Centre Square." I think about the broken windows on the front of Sebastian Labs and wonder if Harold's patient from this story did it. "Afterwards, father thought it best for me to stay home. He said Mother had become too weak to travel back and forth and I needed to stay with her and give her blood transfusions to slow her turning. But to be honest, his eyes told me something else."

"What do you mean by that?" Andrew asks.

"I think he was fearful. The results weren't exactly what he expected. It caught him off guard. Likely more for our protection." Carissa pauses as if the story weighs on her. "I'm sure he had to have done more experiments. Anyway, I'm sure this is what happened to Emily."

"So, now what do we do?" Andrew asks.

"We have to go find her," I say without reservation.

"I agree, but what if she isn't Emily? Inside?" Andrew points to his head. "I mean, we don't know what she's become. You saw that mess she left in the hallway. There's nothing left of Bertha. And what about the door? The knob and the scratches. And... and, if that was her, she's out in the daylight. Does it mean she's not a Vampire anymore or is she just dealing with the pain? If that's the case, then aren't you worried she may not be herself?"

"I hadn't thought about that," I say out loud, more to myself, as the thought blankets me in uncertainty. I shake the thoughts away.

"Well, it doesn't matter who she becomes, it's still Emily. We owe it to her to find out. What if there's something left inside her? A little Emily is better than no Emily."

"You're right, but how do we even know where to look?" Andrew asks.

I'm struck without an answer. If it's true that she's become this thing, then she could be anywhere. But, if Emily is in there somewhere, then my guess is she's going to go to a place familiar to her. I answer, "I think we start back at the house. Maybe something inside of her may want to go home. We'll start there."

"You're not going without me," Carissa chirps, trying to sound confident, but falling short as her voice wavers.

I snicker at her and continue planning with Andrew. "So, we're going to need whatever weapons we have. Pack the duffel bag with everything. We'll take the Camaro and –"

"Excuse me!" Carissa interrupts with frustration spilling from her voice. "I said you aren't going without me."

"You were serious?" Andrew laughs. Starsky lets out a whimper, sounding like a hyena mimicking Andrew.

"Of course I'm serious."

"Carissa, c'mon. You don't belong out there," I say.

She stomps her foot like a child who isn't getting her way, "What do you mean I don't belong out there?"

"Look, you are the reason we are in this situation to begin with. No offense, but you don't have good judgement. Nearly every single decision since we've met you has been a poor decision. One decision after another," Andrew states the facts.

"Not everything was my fault. You can't control everything out there. It's an apocalyptic jungle," she argues.

"That's true. You can't control everything," I say. "But the difference between life and death is the decision you make *in* that jungle. We've survived because we make excellent decisions when our lives are on the line. Don't you think if we go looking for Emily, it would be safer for all of us if you just stayed here? Emily would agree."

"Look," she declares, slowing down her speech. "I've come a long way since Emily first trained me. I admit I'm rough around the edges, but with Emily, I've come so far. Yes, I panicked, but I won't do it again. I promise. Emily and I connected. And I feel like I owe it to her to help."

I look at Andrew, and he throws up his hands like he gives up.

As darkness settles, we complete our plans or what's a loose interpretation of a plan like faint lines from an erased chalkboard. When we go up against Feasters, we can control things. With humans, there's more of a challenge because they aren't so mindless, but at least you can reason with them. I don't feel as confident going up against whatever Carissa thinks Emily has turned into. If she's capable of doing what she did to Bertha, we may be in way over our heads. I hope we can reason with her, bring her home, and help her get through this.

Chapter 13

Fireflies

At dark, the three of us and Starsky pile into the Camaro. Andrew and I decide to head over to the house. I know our house is an empty shell, but it's a place that holds memories for the three of us. Emily may choose to go there. Another choice would be Emily's old house, but we haven't been back there since the early days of the apocalypse. Because both houses are close to each other, we can easily sweep the area to look for her. Besides, there are other supplies Emily and I left behind when we went back and found Starsky. So, if Emily isn't here, we can get the rest of the items from the garage.

I make the headlights of the Camaro go dark about a block away. With the Camaro crawling through the street towards the cul-de-sac, the three of us search out of the windows looking for any signs of Emily. There's nothing but a few stray Feasters. I turn the car around so it's facing away from the cul-de-sac in case we need to make a quick getaway.

We exit the car and walk up to the house without making a sound. By looking at Andrew's face, I can tell he's feeling what Emily and I were feeling when we first saw the charred remains of our home.

He looks down at Starsky and clicks his tongue, sending Starsky to sniff around.

"What's he doing?" I ask Andrew as I watch Starsky, his nose to the ground.

"He's just checking if Emily was here."

"Man, that's a cool power."

"It's good, and I think I'm getting better at controlling it." Starsky stops by the melted mess of Feasters on the front lawn. He circles and then sits down, pawing at the air. "He's found something."

"More Feasters?" Carissa wonders, fear causing any attempt at bravery in her voice to waver.

"I don't think so," Andrew responds.

It's then that Carissa gets a good look at what used to be our home. "Are... are we responsible for this? My father and me?"

I gaze upon the charred home, my lips pursing together. "More or less. It wasn't burning when you left."

"But how?"

"That's not important right now." My focus shifts to Starsky. Andrew is at his side. "What is it?"

"Emily was here, but I don't know if it's an old odor Starsky smells or something fresh. Let's head inside."

"You sure you want to? It's not pretty in there," I remind Andrew.

"It ain't pretty out here either. We've got to see if she was here. Any kind of clue."

We head past the mound of melted Feasters on the lawn. By now the smoldering has stopped, and stench replaces it, forcing us to cover our faces to escape the smell. Their groans grow more excited as we pass. Even Starsky takes a wide pass around them.

We cross the threshold into the house. Carissa pulls out three battery powered lanterns and sets them on remnants of a table that survived the fire. The three of us look for any sign of Emily, but honestly, I'm not even sure what we're looking for besides Emily herself. We move through the living room into the kitchen. Andrew notices the basement door is open and grabs one lantern. "I'm gonna go down and look," Andrew says. In anticipation of what he will find, his eyes well up in the corners. It's funny. I'm not surprised Andrew has the gift he has. The kid always connected with our animals. Starsky. Hutch. Mr. Pickles. Even the goat. They always flocked around him well before he realized his ability to communicate with them. I know when he sees the three of them down there, he's going to need a shoulder. From downstairs he calls, "Hey Kieran? You're gonna want to come down here."

I purse my lips, confused, wondering if he just doesn't want to cry in front of Carissa. I look at her. "Give me a minute."

"Of course. I'll just look around if you don't mind."

I nod my head and make my way down to the basement, noticing right away Hutch is no longer there. Andrew is standing at

the bottom of the steps. "Didn't you say our animals were down here?"
I nod. "Well, they're gone. Hutch. The goat. Ms. Pickles. Gone."

"Well, I assure you they were here the other day. Where did they go?"

"Feasters? That's not possible. Dogs? Other animals?" Andrew asks. I know we've seen some dogs prowling in the night. I'm sure they used to be family pets at one point or another. But now, with no one to feed them, they eat the scraps the Feasters or any other living things leave behind. I'm sure they've learned how to hunt by now, too. I remember learning something about how animals adapt to their environment. The more I think about it, the more this idea doesn't sound too far-fetched. So where are they?

Carissa's excited voice interrupts my thoughts. "Hey boys? Boys, come look at this."

Andrew and I shoot confused glances at each other before bolting up the stairs. We find Carissa, hands cupped around her eyes, looking out of the window of the door leading to the backyard. "What is it? Do you see her?" Andrew asks, his voice teetering somewhere between concern and excitement.

"No, I don't. Fireflies. It's amazing! Tons of them." She takes a break from looking at them to see us, a child's joy plastered across her face. "It's so beautiful!"

We rush to her side and look through the glass. Sure enough. Hundreds. No, thousands of them hovering in the air, flashing their lights. It's then I look up at the top window of the door and see a massive bloody handprint. "Look at that!" Wonder encapsulates my breath as I point up to direct Andrew's attention.

Andrew's eyes widen. "Emily?"

"I don't know, but have you seen a handprint that big before?"

"Nope, just like we've seen nothing as big as what Emily may have turned into." Andrew and Carissa force a smile that isn't quite a smile but more nervous and bewildered, and the excitement about fireflies is short-lived. Now the uncertainty of what is in the backyard among those fireflies looms darker. "Should we go outside and look?" I ask.

"Out there?" Carissa's voice wavers.

"We came here to find Emily. If she's out there, we need to find out," Andrew tries to reassure Carissa.

"Yeah, so let's do it. Carissa, stand behind us until Andrew and I can see if the coast is clear."

She shoots her shoulders back in an effort of confidence. "This girl can handle herself in a fight," she whispers.

"Carissa. We aren't fighting the dead. You said it yourself. Emily may be half dead, but whatever else she's become, I'm not sure it's the fight you want."

Her shoulders slump a bit, but she fights to hold onto her confidence. "Well, I'm not going to let you do all the dirty work."

Andrew laughs. "Well, that's the spirit." He pats Carissa on the back.

I take on a more serious tone, "Hey, are we going to check out the backyard or what?"

"Lead the way," Andrew chuckles, putting his hand out, inviting me to go first.

As we walk down the porch steps, I look back and notice Carissa is staying back. It's clear that fear overwhelms her. I nod at her to let her know it's okay. Directing my attention to the backyard, my stomach flutters with nerves. The fireflies tickle our faces as they land on us or flutter past our exposed skin, encouraging us to move further into the backyard. Around the cedar tree, the fireflies circle around it in unison.

"Look," Andrew points to the ground. Next to the tree, three small graves, two bigger and one smaller, lay next to each other, a cross, woven of sticks and fastened with strands of taller grass, sticks into the ground. "What's buried there?"

"I don't know," I say. The graves are too small to be human. Children? Unlikely. Then it hits me all at once. "They're graves for our animals."

"Did you do this?" Andrew asks.

"No. We found Starsky and beelined it out of here," I say, kneeling to get a closer look at the graves. "Look at this." Claw marks etch into the ground. "These graves weren't dug with a shovel."

"How do you know?"

"Have you ever been to the beach or dug holes at a playground? You use your hands to dig the hole, right?"

"Yeah, the hole is never even and has handprints and lines from your fingers," Andrew's eyes light up as if a pleasant memory rushes into his head.

"Right. Look right here." I move out of the way so the lantern can shine on what I'm talking about. "See, around the edges of each grave? These are marks made by hands, except these aren't just any old hands. Look how deep they carve into the ground. The dirt isn't exactly soft. Emily must still be whatever she turned into at Sebastian Labs."

"Emily?" Andrew questions.

"That's my guess. It's possible she came back here to bury our animals." Andrew nods. "You know what this means." Excitement hits me.

"That Emily is going to need a manicure in a bad way?" Andrew laughs.

"No. Well, probably. But seriously, this means there's enough of Emily left inside the beast she's become. Emily's still in there."

"Yeah, that makes sense!"

It's then I notice something's different. "Hey, where'd the fireflies go?"

Andrew stands up straight, looks up to the sky, and spins around, scanning the yard for them. "Huh, they were here a second ago." He turns towards the house. "Hey, Carissa. Did you see –? Where'd she go?"

I gaze at the house. The back door is open where she was, but only Carissa's backpack is in the doorway. "Carissa? Where'd you go?" I call out to her.

"Maybe she went inside. She may have felt safer."

From the front of the house, we hear tires squeal. By the time the three of us race inside, through the burnt out remains of what used to be the living room, we see the black van whipping a one eighty and hustling down the block. Starsky, sensing our excitement, starts barking. "It's the van from the other night!" Andrew yells.

"They've got to have Carissa! Dang it!" I throw a fist into my open hand.

Starsky's barking shifts to a low growl. "What's the matter, boy?"

Two large Feasters approach the opening in front of the house and stop. The bigger of the two lifts his arms in the air. Then, shadows of dozens of Feasters rows deep make their way towards the house, entering through the threshold and the gaping hole burned out in front of the home where the bay window once was. Their groans intensify with the prospect of a meal. As they approach, more replace the droves coming in. The smell, now a mixture of ash, smoke, and the remains of rotting flesh, fills our senses. We stand paralyzed, momentarily, before Starsky's ferocious barks snap us to our senses.

My blood races through my body as I transform. I ready my machete and Andrew lifts his bat. Our eyes blaze red, and our fangs drop as we set off to fight our way through. I slice my blade through two Feasters' skulls. Spinning off that move, I crouch and hobble the next one, a large, bearded zombie. Andrew brings the bat down onto his zombie's head, collapsing the skull and sending his brains splattering. He takes the handle of the bat and drives it through the throat of the next one. It sprawls backwards into the Feaster behind it. I take my blade and melt it through the top of its head, splitting the skull and half down through the neck as the ones next to it reach and claw at our clothes.

Andrew yells, "Kieran, there are too many of them. We've gotta move."

As the next one stalks dangerously close, my machete impales the female Feaster through the eyes and comes out the other side. "What about Carissa?"

"We'll be no help to her if we're dead. We can just slip out the side gate. Like the good old times."

"Good idea!"

As we move towards the back door for our escape, Andrew trips over a dead Feaster and falls hard on his back. The next Feaster moves to make a meal out of Andrew. Starsky, sensing his distress, bounds up and hits the Feaster in the chest with his body, sending him upright. I swing my machete and decapitate it. I grab Andrew by his collar and Starsky grabs hold of Andrew's pant leg, and we drag him through the back door. As I struggle to catch my breath, the door slams shut, and we scurry down the stairs. "You good?" I ask.

"Yeah, that was close. Stupid leg! I wish it would heal already. I can communicate with animals, but I can't heal a hundred percent? Sheesh!"

Silhouettes of Feasters scratch and pound on the glass, begging to come outside and play with their food. As Andrew and I ready ourselves to move around the house, a scream comes from inside the house, freezing us in our tracks. Starsky sniffs the air as if a fresh scent fills his senses. Without warning, the splattering of zombie blood and brains sprays across the windows as silhouettes of bodies fall to the ground. Other Feasters catapult into the air and smash into walls with thuds shaking the house. Something lifts another one into the air and in an instant, shreds it in two, adding to the red dripping down the windows of the kitchen. CRASH! Two more bodies, one after another, come through the window of the door leading to the steps. One lands on the stairs; the other lays limp halfway through the window, its skull split with shards of glass impaled into exposed brains. Then, silence. We listen for what feels like a lifetime. Our eyes wide and hearts pounding. Starsky's tail hides between his legs, and his body is wrapped around Andrew's. Finally, a large shadow moves past the broken windows and in a flash, it's gone.

"What in the world?!" Andrew whispers in wonder.

Shaking my head in disbelief, I think about what to say, but explanation escapes me. "I have no idea. I've never seen anything clear out a herd with such quickness..."

"And with such brutality." Andrew manages an awkward, nervous chuckle. He walks toward the stairs apprehensively. The screen door was ripped off its hinges from the zombie projectile. When he gets to the top of the steps and looks in, he turns back to look at me with amazement plastered across his face. "Kieran, you've gotta see this." I rush to his side and peer over the Feaster hanging out of the window of the door and into the kitchen. Pushing open the door with the zombie still hanging through, Andrew, Starsky, and I see bodies and limbs smeared and splattered throughout the kitchen and into the charred out remains of the living room. Andrew chuckles, "Man, there goes the resale value. Did Emily do this?"

"I'm wondering the same thing."

"What do we do now?" Andrew asks, scratching Starsky's ears.

I walk over the bodies into the middle of the kitchen and turn around to face Andrew. I throw my hands up in the air, "It looks like Emily's got things handled and can obviously take care of herself. And, I have a feeling she's not very far off. We need to go find out what happened to Carissa. If that's the same van that was outside Carissa's house and followed us after we found Starsky, then we gotta go after it."

"Remember how they wanted Carissa?" Andrew remembers.

"Yeah, well, they got her. You know what we have to do?"

"Yup. Let's get her back," Andrew's voice turns serious.

As we rush through the house, I notice one of the large Feasters mutilated on the front lawn. In his hand, lies a machete not much different from my own. "Since when do Feasters carry around weapons? What the heck are we up against?" I reach down and pry the machete from his hand and take a second to test its weight and balance. I look at Andrew and joke, "He won't be needing this anymore."

We take down the few Feaster stragglers as we rush to the Camaro. I throw the car into gear and race down the block. "Where are we going?" Andrew wonders.

"The place where Emily and I followed the black van. I'm positive they took her there." It's funny because right now, it's the only thing I'm sure about. What we're up against can't even be real. Feasters who can lead other Feasters? Feasters that rely on weapons? As if fighting the dead wasn't challenging enough. Can these Feasters really follow commands? That's next level fear. Without Emily by our side, I'm not sure if Andrew, Starsky, and I will have what it takes to rescue Carissa. I'm praying that somewhere; Emily is close by and ready if we need her because right now, we don't know what we are up against.

Chapter 14

Another Rescue Run

A steady fog rolls in with a chill in the night air as we approach the darkened warehouse, which looks more like one of those haunted houses our families loved taking us to when we were younger during Halloween. The fog casts twisted shadows over the Feasters inside the gates, meandering like disorganized guards bumping into each other, overseeing the fences. The black van rests in front of a door. An oversized garage door takes up most of the side of the building.

"The last time we were here," I whisper to Andrew, "Emily and I crept along that fence lining the building. There are a few windows, but not a lot of places to get in. Just more doors like that one."

"What about up there?" Andrew points. At the corner of the building is a steel ladder attached to a fire escape that reaches to the roof. "I bet they wouldn't expect that, right?"

"How do we know it's not all locked up?"

"It doesn't matter. I brought these," Andrew bounces his eyebrows while holding a pair of bolt cutters and our crowbar. "Just like every other lock we've popped."

"Starsky won't be able to get up there."

"I've got other plans for him. Are you ready?" I nod to him. Starsky kisses Andrew's face as he kneels down to him. Starsky embraces Andrew with two massive paws on his shoulders. Andrew, close to Starsky's ear, whispers something which freezes him like he's listening before he showers Andrew's face with kisses again. Starsky sits at his side, anticipating Andrew's next command. He turns to me. "Let's do this." With a click of his tongue, Starsky takes off to the opposite side of the fence line and sits, looking at us. Andrew puts his hand in the air and then drops it, signaling Starsky to shout three loud barks. He continues to do this in choruses of three. One by one, the Feasters inside the gate shamble towards the sound until all of them line up at the fence. Their groans for food are directed at Starsky as he paces from corner to corner. Within minutes, all the Feasters are watching him.

"There's a lot more of them than I thought," I say to Andrew.

"Yeah, I hope that fence holds."

"We better move." Rushing to the other side of the fence behind the bushes Emily and I snuck around on our first trip here, Andrew climbs. "Wait," I whisper. "I think we need an alternate escape route. If we get Carissa out, I'm not sure what shape she'll be in. She may not be able to climb."

"Great idea. You're getting the hang of this leadership thing." Andrew chuckles as I punch him in the arm.

As the fog thickens, he snips the fence along the corner post and peels the chain links back enough for us to get through. We notice now that Starsky has the zombies' attention; he doesn't bark as often, so he doesn't alert whoever or whatever is inside the building. With weapons in hand, we rush to the corner of the building and scoot up the ladder undetected. Like light-footed ninjas, we move to the one access point inside. The hatch isn't locked. I had hoped there would be a door so we would have more control and be ready to fight. The hatch leads to a tight fitting, cave-like tunnel with a ladder built into it. We're forced to move single file and with our weapons holstered. What scares me most is we have little idea of what we'll face when we get to the bottom. These thoughts consume my mind as we start our descent. Luckily, it's clear at the bottom, and when we light one lantern, we find ourselves in a small, closet-sized janitorial closet. I notice containers of floor wax and other cleaning products on shelves. Andrew whispers, "This would have come in handy after you and Emily made that mess saving me."

"Right? Most of the floor is still sticky with Feaster guts." We joke and collect ourselves for what comes next.

I turn the lantern off and turn the handle of the closet door as if it's booby trapped. I pull the door towards me, revealing a dark hallway. Initially, I think about turning on the lantern, but push the thought aside, knowing it would blow our cover. Instead, we let our eyes adjust because as Vamps, we see very well in the dark. We find ourselves at the corner of two hallways. We aren't sure which way to go, so we listen for anything that would lead us in the right direction. Nothing.

Then, without warning, halfway down the hallway, a door opens, revealing the flickering light of a candle or lantern and the shadow of a man filling the space. He steps out into the hallway and walks away from us. Then, he rights his shoulders and stops, craning his neck, looking back in our direction. The heat of my face fills my cheeks. Should we run? Should we fight? The blood pumps through my veins as my Vampire instincts fire. Andrew senses this and cues his own transformation. The man turns around and walks in our direction. Andrew slips back into the janitor's closet, and I move down the other hallway a little. By now, my eyes are burning red in the dark hall and may be the perfect distraction. The man walks to the intersection between the hallways. My eyes provide the only light, floating like UFOs hovering in the sky. "Wh – What the heck?" I hear the man grumble, a slight hint of fear hinging behind his voice. He pauses for a moment, looking like he's deciding what to do. He takes two steps in my direction. Andrew sneaks out of the closet and sweeps his legs with his bat, upending him so his body hits the ground with a thump. Without hesitation, I move towards him as Andrew takes his ankles and flips him so he's face down. Before he realizes it, I reach my arm across his neck and secure it with my other arm. Although he struggles for a moment, it isn't long before he passes out. I roll over onto my back and take a second to catch my breath. Adrenaline pumps blood through my body. Andrew and I each grab a leg and drag him into the closet. Out of his backpack, Andrew grabs the duct tape we always carry and covers the man's mouth over his beard and moustache. "That's gonna hurt coming off," Andrew laughs. I lift the man's ankles and hands and tape them together like we're preparing him for one of those Hawaiian pig roasts. This way, when he comes to, he won't have his limbs to kick against the door. In this place where we're unsure where anything is, we don't need this guy to blow our cover.

Andrew and I have returned to our normal selves. Andrew checks the man's pockets. We find one of those handheld stun guns and two keys secured to his pant loops. Andrew jokes, "Maybe this is the janitor, and this *is his* closet."

"Then he'll feel right at home. Let's do this."

Sneaking down the hallway, Andrew peers into the room where the guy came out of. He exits with his finger pinching his nose and his face looking like he just ate a lemon.

"What's in there?" I whisper, my eyes fixed on Andrew's contorted face.

"You don't wanna know. Whatever that guy ate died inside of him and forced its way out! So gross."

I stifle a laugh. "Better you than me. Let's go."

Creeping down the hallway, we find no signs of life until we get to the end. We hear the same familiar reggae song I heard in the dream where I saw my mother. I can't put my finger on how I know it. Besides the music, faint voices come from a room with light shining out of the space at the bottom. Moving closer, the light and the voices aren't the only things we sense. The rotting stench of Feaster flesh fills the hallway.

Andrew pinches his nose. "Feasters?" I nod my head, my eyes flushed with concern. As we approach the room, the voices of men become clearer and so does the smell of decaying flesh. We can't tell whether it's coming from the room or further down the hallway. Deciding to investigate, we pass the door and creep further down.

The smell intensifies as we get closer to a door at the end. Andrew tries the door, but it's locked. He remembers the keys we took from the guy we put in the janitor's closet. On the first try, the key slips into the keyhole. The grotesque smell smacks us in the face. Inside looks like a factory break room, complete with several dusty round tables and chairs in their places and a bulletin board with faded memos stapled to it announcing the company picnic. A picnic which likely didn't happen. The smell intensifies, and so does the sound of Feasters. Their groans and growls fill the room and vibrate the door labeled Warehouse. "That sounds like a lot of them!"

"You think? Who are these people?" I look around the room and see a row of windows line the wall a foot above the door. We jump onto the counter and peer inside.

"What in the world!?" Andrew and I say in wonder.

Inside, hundreds of Feasters with different levels of decay shuffle with no direction or purpose around the large warehouse. Their deteriorated faces call out in desperation for food and blood. From different places on the ceiling in the warehouse, heavy chains dangle with thick metal hooks. My father was a bit of a car junkie; these hooks hanging around the warehouse remind me of the pulleys he used to lift heavy engines in and out of cars. The hobby of repairing and restoring old cars was an escape for him. An escape from the prejudice he experienced. Somehow, I think he felt restoring these old cars was a lot like trying to change the minds of those who were stuck in old beliefs about us – about Vampires. Well, at least that's what my mother would say. Chills race down my spine when I notice what appears to be the carcass of an animal hanging on one of the hooks. Only ligaments holding the bones together remain. Beneath the carcass, a group of Feasters kneel in a huddle, savagely feasting on whatever was left of the offering.

"They're feeding them?!" I ask in disbelief.

"What are they feeding them?" Andrew asks, and a shakiness accompanies his voice.

"I don't know. These people are crazy. We need to get Carissa and get out of here."

After getting down, I start toward the door. Andrew grabs me by the arm. "Hey Kier, about Carissa." He's struggling with the words to say.

"Yeah, what about her?" I notice his hands are shaking.

"To be honest, Kieran. I'm scared. This feels bigger than you. Me. Emily. We don't owe Carissa anything. It's obvious this group of people will do whatever it takes to get their hands on her. They want her. Not us. It wouldn't surprise me if it has something to do with Sebastian Labs. We can't be the only ones that place has done something wrong to."

"What are you saying, Andrew?"

He looks down at his feet. "I'm saying, let's get out of here. Go find Emily and just stick to what we do best. Caring for each other. Things were simpler when it was just us and our animals, right? We tried this whole *finding others* thing, and it's not all it's cracked up to be."

"So, we just leave Carissa? What if they hurt her?" On one hand, I'm surprised to hear this from Andrew. When he came into our lives, we didn't just leave him to die. We saved his life and welcomed him into the family. But, on the other hand, I get it. He's scared. So am I. He has some good points. Life was easier before all this. We made the promise to Harold to care for her, but when is it okay to break this promise? When our lives are in danger? Our lives haven't fared better since that ill-fated night. In fact, they've been a heck of a lot worse. But I don't think we could live with ourselves without trying to rescue Carissa. What if they hurt her or even worse? I don't think this is what Emily would want either, regardless of her feelings about Carissa.

"Kieran, I get it. It would be horrible, but they have an entire warehouse full of Feasters they can control. This is impossible," he pleads, his eyes bloodshot and pained.

"Andrew, I don't care how bad things are, if Carissa dies, and we did nothing about it when we could have, it will destroy you and me, right here," I say while pointing to his heart. "I'm scared too. But we have to at least try something." Andrew drops his head as teardrops fall from his eyes, making tiny puddles on the concrete floor. "I promise you this. If it gets to a point where it gets too much to handle, we cut and run. Go back to the drawing board. We just can't leave Carissa without trying. Deal?"

Andrew nods his head. I give him a hug and a second to gather himself. We sneak out of the break room. As I'm silently pulling the door shut, I hear a THWACK! Out of the corner of my eye, I see Andrew fall to the ground. I spin to see what happened and the last thing I see is a plank of wood coming towards me. THWACK! I see a man standing over me before everything goes black.

Chapter 15

Family Reunion

I'm spinning. Spinning and spiraling. Out of control, I'm whirling. I try to get my bearings, but it's no use. Falling fast. Finally, my body lands softly in the corner of a room that feels familiar. My eyes struggle to find out where I am. Sitting up, I find myself in my bedroom. The bedroom I had growing up. Glancing out of my tinted window, cars rest parked on streets and on driveways like they were before they are now. The streets are clean and free from the carcasses of humans, Vampires, and Feasters. The world is back to how things used to be, but something lurks beneath the surface. This day feels familiar. When I hear a knock at my door and see my father enter, it floods back. A range of emotions swell over me. I've missed him, so seeing him after what feels like forever excites me. I want to jump into his arms and feel his embrace. However, this day is the day he tells me my mother has died. I recognize the look on his face, and I shake my head, not wanting to relive it over again.

Glancing over to my bed, I see a younger me. My father sits on the edge of my bed, collecting his thoughts. "Son," he whispers to me. Emotions choke his words. "I want to talk to you about your mother."

"What's the matter, Dad?" I ask.

"She's been in an accident."

"Is she okay? Why didn't you call me? I'm sure Marlene would have taken me there." Marlene, my older cousin, was the one who watched me if my parents had to work or needed a night out. "When is she coming home?"

I watch my father's shoulders sink and then heave, as a tsunami of emotion overwhelms his body. My own eyes watch the scene play out. It's the same scene I've played in my mind repeatedly. I recall the odd sight of such a hulking man reduced to rubble by his emotions. He pulls me close and embraces me into his chest. "She's not coming home, buddy." After what feels like ages, he peels himself from me and looks me in the eye. From the corner of the room, I mouth the words as he says it to the younger me. "Your mother was so proud of you. She'd want you to be strong and stay true to yourself." Watching the scene, my heart breaks. Having to relive this moment again is unfair, but seeing my father again balances my feelings.

Then, my father gets up from the bed and looks at me from where I'm standing in the dream. "Hello, Kieran," his voice echoes as if broadcasting from a different place. I'm shocked he's talking to me. I look over to the bed, and I'm surprised to see my younger self staring at me. My father walks over, his body still much larger than mine. "Look at how much you've grown." His warm hands cup my face, and with his thumbs, he swipes the tears streaming from my eyes.

"How is this possible? Am I dead?"

"No son," he chuckles. His voice echoes, filling the room. "Quite the opposite."

"Then why is this happening?"

"Your mother, son. She was the strongest of us all. We always believed you would lead us some day."

"Me? I'm just a kid."

He chuckles, "Age doesn't make a leader. Heart does. You've always had the heart."

"I don't feel like that sometimes. If it wasn't for Emily, I may have already given up."

"But we both know you wouldn't." I know that to be the truth, but it's so hard sometimes. Then, my father puts both hands on my shoulders. "Son, the night she died, she wanted me to give this to you, but I was so overcome with her loss, I never did." He fishes something out of his pocket. It's a thick leather square about two inches on each side. Branded in red on one side is a circle with a triangle in it, with the points poking outside the circle. My fingers trace the shapes. Turning it over, I read in my mother's handwriting, *You will lead us!*

"Dad, what does this mean?" I ask, shaking my head. "And what is this symbol?"

"Your mother assured me you would know what it means when the time comes." He smiles down on me without parting his lips. "I have to go."

"No, you can't go now. I have so many questions."

"You will get the answers you need in time," his voice echoes.

"Dad? I've missed you."

"I know, kiddo. I've missed you too." He touches my cheek and leaves the room.

I look around, and I am alone. I turn over the leather square several times in my hands, trying to piece together what's happened.

Without warning, I'm spinning again. Spinning. Spiraling. Until I splash down, and I wake up struggling to make sense of my surroundings. My face is dripping wet. I try to move my hands to wipe the water from my eyes, but I can't move them. It only takes a second to realize my hands are secured behind my back. Searching around the room, I try to figure out where I am. The last thing I remember is seeing a room full of Feasters. Yes, I remember. We were rescuing Carissa. We? Andrew. I look to my left, and he's also bound and unconscious. A wave of pain overcomes my head. That's right! Someone hit me.

Splash! I gaze over to Andrew, and he's dripping with water, too. "Get up! Both of you!" a voice demands. Standing over us is a man, a bucket hanging from his hand. "Let's go. Time to wake up." I struggle to my knees and see Andrew stir. "That's it. Get up!"

"Okay, okay," I manage, the pain in my head increasing as I get upright. "Give us a second." I look over at Andrew. "Hey, are you okay?"

"Kieran? What's happening? I can't move my hands."

"Take a second, buddy. Someone captured us." I'm surprised at how calm I feel.

"Captured? Did we break the law or something?" Andrew mutters, getting to his knees.

"Something like that, except I don't think this guy is a police officer. If he is, he's pretty out of shape," I say as he comes into focus.

"Well, round is a shape," Andrew jokes, and then the pain hits him. "Oh man, my head hurts. What the heck happened?"

"You two need to shut up, right now." The man comes into focus. He's a round man in a thick coat whose buttons struggle to hold on. His greying beard, a scraggly mess across his face.

"Are you the one who hit us? It takes a real man to hit a guy when his back is turned." I say, putting together the pieces of what happened.

"Is this the guy?" Andrew asks in his wise guy voice. "Before this night is through, you will get the worst wedgie of your life."

"Where's Carissa?" I shout.

"The girl?" the man grumbles. "You two have bigger issues to worry about."

"Well, you'd know the meaning of bigger," Andrew laughs.

"Why, you little –"

Before the Feasters took over, I'd never entertain the thought of using my Vampire powers to get the upper hand on someone or to threaten, but these times are different. "Listen, sir. I'm sure you are a reasonable person. I don't think you recognize what you're up against. You don't want us to get more upset than we already are. We're not like others."

"He's not wrong, Chunk," Andrew chimes in.

The man stalks toward us, sweat dripping from his beard. "Is that so? Well, I think it's you two that don't know who you're messing with." As he moves close to us, his eyes shine a deep crimson color, catching Andrew and me off guard.

"Vampire?" I whisper, confused.

"Stand down, Milo," a booming voice sounds from the shadows of a doorway.

"Yeah, Milo. I guess we all know you're not in charge. Shocker," Andrew turns up the sass. Milo shoots us a stern glance. Andrew fires a wink right back, which causes Milo to grumble some more.

Milo steps back several steps as the man from the doorway, flanked by two others, a man and woman, walk into the light. My mouth drops open in shock as I recognize the large man in the middle. "Dad?"

Chapter 16

Unique is My Dove

I was sure my father was walking with the dead after the night the Feasters wiped out my family. Each night, I looked for him. Each night I held onto hope I would at least see him with them. It wasn't the fate I would ever want for him or anyone for that matter, but my heart ached to know what happened to him.

So, as he walks through the shadow and into the light, I'm confused... and upset... and elated. Regardless of the hope I held in my heart, as time pressed on, I never thought this a possibility. Not for a second. I call his name and wait, holding my breath for what feels like forever for him to respond. So, when he responds, "Kieran? How? Where?" He shakes his head, disbelieving, before willing his body to reach out. Rushing to my side, he unbuckles the buck knife fastened behind him and cuts through the thick tape securing my wrists and pulls me to his chest. I can feel his breath and his tears against my skin and know nothing has ever felt so good. He peels himself from me and looks into my eyes. "Kieran, I can't believe it's you. How long? What happened? I have so many questions."

"Ha," I laugh with relief from my chest. "You have questions? Seriously? I have plenty of my own."

"Um, I have questions, too. Actually, just one. Can someone set me free? I can't feel my fingers and my head is killing me," Andrew says, pleading.

"May I?" I ask my dad, taking his knife from him and freeing Andrew. I help him to his feet and hug him. "Andrew, this is... this is my father."

"Whoa! Nice to meet you, sir."

With tears in his eyes, he looks to me, then to Andrew, and back to me. "I... I don't know how this is possible."

"You're telling me? Dad, that night Emily and I saw your body lying in the doorway. We thought you were dead. Or worse. Aunt Rosemary told us to run and find shelter. So, we did what we were told. When we got the nerve to come back to see if there were any survivors and to salvage supplies, you weren't there. Emily and I were sure you were out there walking with the Feasters."

My dad stares into my eyes, entrenched in the story. "Feasters?"

"That's what we call them, sir," Andrew chimes in. "On account they are always looking for a meal. Kinda like Chunk over there. Am I right?" Andrew winks at Milo.

Milo bites, "You little punk, I'll –"

My father puts his hand up, and Milo goes silent. "Go on," he urges.

"I'm not sure what else to say. Every time we are out there against the Feasters, I always inspect their faces to see if one of them is you. God, I've missed you." I lunge in for a hug.

"Well, you don't have to search any longer. I'm here, son."

"What happened to you?"

"Honestly, my memory is still hazy from that night. I remember the chaos. I remember watching our injured and dead family members attack each other. Chaos. Screaming. Ripping. Growling. The splattering of blood. I pulled one of them off someone. I can't remember who. It was all very confusing. When I pulled that thing off, it spun around. It's *eyes*… I still have nightmares. It lunged for me, and I lost my balance and the back of my head hit something and I was out cold." He stares off in the distance, as if the story still rests at the surface and then regains his focus. "Emily? You said you were with Emily. Where is she?" He gulps hard, dreading the answer.

"It's a long story. We don't know where she is." My father looks over to Andrew for confirmation, and he nods. "Hundreds of Feasters cornered us on this cul-de-sac," my voice trails off as it hits me. The van. The Feasters.

He notices my change in demeanor, "What's wrong?"

"That van outside. It brought those Feasters to us." I watch as the two people flanking my father shoot knowing glances at each other. "Where's Carissa? That van took off with her when we were back at the house. Where is she?" My voice takes on an urgent and protective tone.

My father looks stunned in disbelief. His eyes flit back and forth, searching for an answer. "That was you? Son, you must believe me, I didn't know you or Emily or Andrew were there. We would never… we just wanted the girl."

"She has a name. It's Carissa," I say, frustration at the tip of my tongue.

The woman standing on my father's left cuts in, "We know exactly who she is. She's a Croger."

Again, my father puts his hand up, and she rolls her eyes in frustration and goes silent. "Son, it's obvious you have developed some kind of bond or friendship with her. Why else would you break in and risk your lives?"

"Risk our lives? Are we in danger here?" Andrew asks, his voice becoming shaky.

"Well, you aren't any longer," my father reassures.

"We want to see Carissa," my voice burns hot.

My father shoots thoughtful glances around the room. He looks over to the woman. She shakes her head, begging for him not to agree. "Okay, you can see her, but we need to talk first."

"What is there to talk about? You're holding a kid hostage, Dad."

"Oh Kieran, there's so much more to her. That family." I know he's talking about Carissa's father, Sebastian Labs, and the cure, but I'm confused because my father would never do something like this.

He's always looked out for Vampires and people alike. I'm not sure how much I should tell him I know.

"Okay," I say. "Let's talk."

"Alone?" Dad suggests.

"Dad, really, anything you have to say about Carissa, Andrew can hear. He probably needs information too."

"Kieran, can't a dad catch up with his son? I'd really appreciate it if we talked alone."

I look over at Andrew. He smiles and nods his head. "Am I going to be safe with Meatball over there?" He points to Milo. "I'm guessing by the lump on my head, he's got some anger issues. I'd feel more comfortable with my baby."

"Baby?" my father asks, confused.

"His bat. It's his baby. It's an unhealthy relationship," I laugh. "Come to think of it, I'd like my machete as well."

"You two are safe here," the man flanking my father replies gruffly.

I stare at the man without breaking eye contact, allowing my eyes to glow red for what feels like minutes. My father breaks the tension, "If they'll feel safer, give the boys their weapons." The two at my father's side hand us our weapons. "And, Milo, step out of the room. I'll call when I need you."

Milo looks frustrated and angry. He looks us over and before he exits the room, Andrew calls, "Hey, Milo? I'm serious about that wedgie!" I try to stifle a chuckle. Even my father cracks a smile. "What? It's gonna happen." Andrew throws up his hands.

The man is going to get his wedgie; I have no doubts. It's going to be pretty funny when it happens. My father moves to walk out of the room and looks back, nodding his head for me to follow. "I'll be back. Okay, pal?" I say to Andrew. "Maybe you two can get him something for his head. It's obvious you have a generator. I bet you have some ice."

My father waits at the door and looks back to his people. "Get the kid an ice pack from a first aid kit and anything else he needs."

We enter the room just across the hall. It's a lit room with a few candles casting more dancing shadows than light onto its walls. A small double sized bed sits in the corner with a few other necessities. What stands out is the music playing. It's the familiar song I heard earlier and the one in my dreams. When my father turns to me, the memory of why this song sounds so familiar unfolds. "This song. It's yours and mom's song, right?"

My father laughs, "Good memory! The first time I heard it, it reminded me of your mother so much. Especially when he sings, 'When I lose my focus, you remind me of the truth.' Matisyahu was our favorite."

"Yeah, I remember now. You guys would go to see him all the time. I feel like reggae music played as the constant soundtrack in our house for a while. What was the name of this song?"

"*Unique is My Dove*. Mom would always roll her eyes whenever it played, and I'd grab her and dance and sing it to her."

"Badly, I might add."

This causes my father to laugh from his belly. "We all have our talents, kid."

"But mom, she had a beautiful voice, right? Mom singing to me before bed was one of my favorite memories as a kid." My face frowns for a moment. "Looking back, my biggest regret is I thought I was too old for her to keep singing to me, so eventually, she stopped."

My dad purses his lips. "Well, if there's one thing the zombie apocalypse has taught me is we need to appreciate what's right in front of us. I am so blessed to have found you. I'm never letting go."

As *Unique is My Dove* plays in the background, I think about my mother and the dreams I've had about her. My shoulders straighten as I realized something. "You know, I'm still having dreams."

"I expect you are. It's your gift."

"It's funny. I've dreamt about Mom a lot in the last weeks. My dreams keep taking me back to that night when the Feasters destroyed our family. In each dream, she kept saying to me, 'He's not dead. He's not dead.' I couldn't understand what she was trying to tell me. It felt so... so... cryptic. But now I realize she was talking about you. She was trying to tell me you were the one who wasn't dead."

"Really? Your dreams are still fascinating."

"Oh, Dad, they've become more and more real."

"How so?" He asks, intrigued.

"She gave me something in my dream."

"I don't understand."

I reach into the inside pocket of my coat, pull out the letter, and hand it to him. "I haven't been able to put this down."

As he unfolds it, his eyes widen and drip with emotion. He reads it, and I notice his hands shake and his fingers move as if he's playing the piano. Then he shakes them as if something is crawling on them, looks up, and reveals, "This is the letter I wrote to your mother after she... after she died. How? How did you get this?"

"Like I said, my dreams have become so real. She held this in her hands. When I woke up, it was in *my* hand."

He stumbles back, looking for his bed to sit on as he's staring at the words he wrote to my mother. "Kieran, this is incredible. Your gifts are so powerful." He looks at the letter and then at me. "So, you're aware about the Crogers?"

I purse my lips tightly. "More than I want to."

"Then you know they are dangerous. They tried to eradicate our kind."

"Yes, we found out almost the hard way, but Dad, there aren't any more of them," I tell him.

"What do you mean?"

"Carissa is all that's left," I report, reading his reaction.

"How do you know?"

"Because we watched Harold die," I say his name to assure him I know what I'm talking about.

My father takes this in, his eyes shifting in search for the next thing to say. "You did? What happened?"

"In a nutshell, Andrew, Emily, and I went on a rescue run. We thought we saw someone shining a distress signal. That's when we ran into Harold and Carissa. It turned out they needed little help. They were just setting us up to use the cure to help his wife, who had been bitten."

"Was he using the cure?"

"The cure," I laugh. "It was the cure that nearly killed us. Harold almost drained Andrew of his blood to save his wife."

"Did it work? Is the cure perfected?" He leans in, very interested while asking.

"Hardly. He needed pure Vampire blood."

My father pinches his eyebrows in thought, "Is Andrew not a full Vampire?"

"No, Emily found him. Injured with little chance of making it. So, we had to make the hard choice to change him."

"No permission?"

"No, there wasn't time. It was literally the choice between life and death."

"So, what happened to Harold's wife?"

"Harold needed pure blood, so the experiment failed. When Harold checked on her, he didn't know she turned. She bit him. While Feaster cells tore through his body, he pleaded with us to take care of Carissa."

"And you agreed?"

"We did."

"You were always a good one. Emily too."

"Harold sacrificed himself to help us get out of there. To save Andrew and Carissa, Emily and I had to fight through about thirty Feasters that Harold held captive."

That perks him up. "You know, son. I bet most of those zombies were test subjects. Vampires."

"Yes, Harold told us."

"How did you get through all those zombies?"

"Emily and I channeled the very thing which made humans afraid of us. It felt freeing and scary and –"

"And powerful?" He clenches a fist.

"Yes!" I think about the blood flowing through my veins when I transform. "That's it, Dad. That's all I know. So, what do you plan on doing with Carissa?"

"We need to know what she knows."

"About what?"

"The cure, of course." My father throws up his hand as if the answer is obvious.

"I can tell you right now. Carissa still has access to it."

He sits up, shocked. "How do you know?"

"When you brought those Feasters to us in the cul-de-sac, a Feaster bit Emily. We rushed back to where we were living."

"Sebastian Labs?"

Instead of answering, I continue with the story. "Carissa tried to use the cure with my blood."

"I'm guessing it didn't work."

I go silent, trying to figure out how to answer. "I don't know."

"I don't understand, son. Is she alive or not?"

I think of Carissa's explanation. "I think she's both. She's not dead, but the cure didn't work either. It changed her into something else. Something I've never seen before."

"I have. That night at the cul-de-sac, did you wonder why those Feasters – is that what you called them – didn't attack you?"

"Yes, the ones in front seemed to control them." I wonder.

"Those at the front were part of Harold's failed experiments."

"Harold mentioned that." I replay the night in my head. "Carissa said some of his experiments had escaped or something."

"Three of them."

"Two of them now," I tell him. My father tilts his head in confusion. "Back at the house when you kidnapped Carissa, you sent them in after us. One of the big ones isn't coming back. Neither are the Feasters." I chuckle inwardly.

"Did *you* kill them?"

"Oh, not me or Andrew." I put my hands up. "We didn't see it. Only silhouettes in the window, but the sound terrified us. It was Emily."

"Emily? How do you know?"

"Dad, we've survived together for the last two years. I just know." It's then I make the connection of the fireflies to Emily, but I don't relay that information with my father. Instead, the room grows silent. My father's fingers tap against his leg. "Dad, what's the matter?" I ask, wondering where this conversation is going. I know it must end with seeing Carissa.

"I'm just putting pieces together."

"I don't know what there is to put together. I've told you everything. Aside from Carissa, there's no one left, and it's time to let me see her. I just want to know how she's doing. She's a bit high-strung. I'm sure she's freaking out."

"I don't think it's a good idea, son. Those people. They took everything. From me. From you. From Vampires. Heck, from the world."

"But you said I could see her if we talked –"

"I KNOW WHAT I SAID!" He shouts at me, sending me back a step. Then, through gritted teeth, he bites, "Those people took everything."

I'm taken back by his reaction but won't let it go. "What do you want with Carissa?"

"We have to know what she knows!" he shouts.

"About what?"

"The cure! Her father! Everything!"

"And then what?" I ask.

We're blanketed in awkward silence. I've never seen him like this, and it's concerning. Although I feel blessed we're reunited, my father resembles a shell of the man I remember. I'm unable to put my finger on it, but my gut tells me Carissa may be in danger. The newspaper articles I found in the offices of Sebastian Labs settle into my thoughts. "Dad," I whisper. He looks up, breaking from his thoughts, squeezing his hands together. When he releases them, his hands still have a slight shake to them. "I know about mom and what happened to her and who killed her." I let this sink in. "I read about the accident and Franklin Croger. It was him." The tears drop from him like large raindrops. "It's true those people tried to get rid of us, but mom's accident was just an accident. An unfortunate coincidence."

He drops his head and sprinkles of tears fall to the floor. His shaky hands move to wipe his eyes and nose. "We've never been sure about that. They never apologized or made a public announcement. Here's some irony for you. They try to *cure* Vampires and change them into what, I have no idea. And… and then, he winds up killing the one person who set out to educate humans and bring our two kinds together. No apology. No admission of guilt. Instead, they move forward with their cure."

I move towards him. "Dad, he's dead too. There's no one left except Carissa."

"I know, son," he whispers, defeated.

Without warning, dark thoughts blanket over me like the setting of the sun as each minute grows darker and the day trades for night. I'm not surprised my mother's death still upsets my father, but the grudges he still holds reveal only rage. Yes, rage bubbles under the surface. My thoughts shift to the article about Franklin's murder. The article questioned whether his death had been an act of revenge for the death of my mother. I try to shake the thought out of my mind, but it sticks to me, and I don't know what to do with it. Does my father know anything about Franklin Croger's murder? Or worse, was he involved? Do I approach? Yes, I must. "Dad?"

"Yes, Kieran." His head still hangs.

I gulp hard. "What do you know about Franklin Croger's death?"

My father's head lifts slowly, and his eyes squint. "What do you mean?"

"I read in another article I found at Sebastian Labs that the police suspected his murder could have been revenge for mom's death. And, the letter you wrote to mom, talks about how the others were seeking revenge and you were struggling with it."

"What are you saying?"

I just come out and say it. "Did you have anything to do with Franklin's death?"

My father stands up and leans in. He grabs the letter from the table and reads it over. "Son, this is an adult matter. There are things you simply wouldn't understand."

"I'm not a kid anymore."

My dad takes a second to look me over and a half smile breaks across his face. "Ain't that the truth."

"So, tell me, Dad."

He pauses, calculating his next words. "Son, there's much I have to teach you about how things work in the Vampire world. Revenge is something which must come before The Circle."

"The Circle?" I've heard that before. When? My dream about Emily. She told me The Circle wants Carissa. Something about revenge. My stomach twists into knots.

"The Circle is the council of Vampires. Think of it like a governing body. Decisions like the one you are talking about go through them."

"I've heard of The Circle in my dreams. Is this something you would support? So, what did they decide?"

"Kieran, what The Circle decides is something we may not talk about. It's not a perfect system, but The Circle has served as the backbone for Vampires for centuries. We don't question their authority."

"But revenge, Dad?"

"Son, we've found each other. I will teach you the ways of The Circle. There's so much to learn."

"About murder?"

"Don't let one thing shape your views about something you know nothing about. You want to see Carissa, right? I will let you and your friend see her."

My stomach still sits in knots, unsettled about this information and the kind of Vampire my father has become. I'm not sure what that is, but he's not the man I remember. He's different. Apathetic? I can't quite put my finger on it. As we approach the door, something catches my eye, "What's that?"

"Oh, this? This is the symbol of The Circle." Tacked on the wall is a small red flag with a white circle overlapped with a triangle whose points protrude out of the circle. It's the same symbol my father gave me in my last dream, branded into the leather square with a message from my mother.

The door flies open. "Silas, we've got a problem. You've got to see this."

We rush out of the room and into the one where I left Andrew. My thoughts flood to the worst-case scenario. Instead, we find Milo screaming and his eyes red, "When I get down, I'm going to tear into you, you little punk! Get me down from here!"

Milo's legs are dangling from a hook on the wall by his underwear. I search the room for Andrew. He's sitting on a chair with a mischievous smile plastered on his face. "What? I told him a wedgie was in his future. He's lucky that's all he gets after whacking us on the head. Besides, he came in all puffy telling me he's going to teach me manners someday."

My father's smirk shifts to a stern look as his attention moves to Milo, whose underwear is ripping. "Is this true?"

"I was bringing the kid some ice for his little boo boo." Milo's eyes return to normal.

"Didn't I give you an order to stay out of this room? I told you no harm is to come to them. It's important they feel safe."

"I wasn't planning on hurting him. I just wanted to scare him a little. Sorry," Milo shifts his eyes downward.

"How did that work out for you?" My father reaches for his knife and cuts what's left of Milo's underwear, and he falls in a heap. I shoot a knowing glance over at Andrew, who's wearing a most satisfied smile. He shrugs his shoulders as I shoot him a wink.

"By the way," Andrew admits, "while you are cutting people down, we may or may not have one of your Vampires hogtied in the janitor's closet down the hallway."

My father rolls his eyes at Milo. "Go check that out." Then turning to us, he half-smiles. "Let's go."

Andrew grabs his backpack and bat and rushes to my side and whispers, "Where are we going?"

"To see Carissa." He nods, pleased with the answer.

As he passes Milo who is still gathering himself, Andrew stops and jokes, "Now, we're even. Friends?" Milo just looks him in the eyes and lets out a dull growl. I half expect his eyes to glow again. They don't. He just finishes buckling his pants and walks to the other side of the room, waiting for us to exit.

As we follow my father down the dark hallways, my mind races with wild thoughts. I'm excited to be with my father. It's truly a dream come true in a world that doesn't offer much in the dream fulfillment business anymore. He's different though. I can't put my finger on it, but he's different. I guess we're all different. How can we not be? This world's gone mad. I think the difference is that even though Emily, Andrew, and I may have teetered on the brink of madness or surrender from time to time, we never crossed over to the other side. I'm not so sure about my father. Could it be he's crossed over or at the very least has one foot on each side straddled between survival and madness? Harold crossed over. The way Carissa describes his journey, it doesn't sound all that different from my father's. There's something else in my gut that still pulls the knot tightly. I feel like I'm missing something. Something that's been there all along; I can't see it, only sense it. As he stops in front of the door and unlocks it, I know one thing for sure; we aren't safe here.

Chapter 17

Ta-Da!

"Kieran! Andrew!" Carissa runs to us, leaping into our arms. "I thought I'd never see you two again!"

"What? You doubted us?" Andrew jokes.

I turn to my father who's waiting at the door, "Can you give us some time to catch up?"

He hesitates for a second. I think he won't go along with it, but then he agrees, "That's fine. I... I," he starts. "It's getting late, and daybreak is in about an hour. You need your rest and I'd prefer it if it wasn't here. I'm still kinda old-fashioned," he chuckles awkwardly, scratching the stubble forming on his chin. "I'm sure you two are hungry. There are animals down the end of the hall, the last room on the right. Also, next to this room has a couple of cots to sleep on. It will hold you over until we figure things out."

I chuckle. It's been a long time since I had a parent tell me what to do. Part of me wants to tell him we've survived on our own for a while. The other part of me takes a second to bask in having a parent again. "Okay. We won't be too long. Have a good sleep." He pauses with a half-smile before closing the door.

"So, tell us what happened," Andrew wonders.

"After they took me, I saw all of those Feasters come in and thought you two would never survive. I was so scared for you. Scared for me, too. Those people who snatched me were so mean. One second, I'm watching from the window and the next, I had a hand across my mouth and another one grabbed my legs. When they pulled me out of the house, there were dozens of them waiting to go in after you. Feasters."

"Well, we made it out. Ta-da!" Andrew tries to lighten the mood.

"How?" Carissa asks.

"It wasn't us," I tell her.

"Then who?" Carissa wonders, her eyes widen.

"Emily," I whisper.

"Seriously? How do you know?"

"We just know," Andrew tells her. "She tore right through that horde."

"I was so frightened," Carissa admits.

"You're okay now," I try to reassure her.

"Am I?" Carissa stammers, concern edging in her voice.

"Yeah, Kieran, is she? Are we?" Andrew turns towards me.

I bring my voice down to a whisper and glance at the door, half expecting to see shadows under it. There aren't any. "I'm not sure what's happening. My father is –"

"Your father? What do you mean? I thought your father –" Carissa questions, surprised.

"Me too. It turns out he's alive."

"Ta-da!" Andrew whispers in a hushed tone.

"That's amazing, Kieran. So, what's the problem?"

"He's my father all right, but there's something different about him."

"Well, how can he not be different? I can only imagine what he went through," Carissa observes.

"No, it's not that. I can't put my finger on it, but we have to get you out of here, Carissa. Somewhere safe."

Andrew looks at me confused. "Kieran, I thought... I figured with your father back in the picture everything was, ya know… at least safer. What did you guys talk about?"

"He's changed. The night when Case bit Emily? My father was there. He's got this revenge thing about Carissa's family."

"My family?"

"The cure. Apparently, there was a lot more than we know happening at Sebastian Labs and their feelings towards Vampires. He's got his mind set on revenge against you and your family."

"But... but I'm just a kid. I knew nothing," she cries in a panicked whisper.

"I told him there was no one left. Only you."

"What did he say?" Andrew asks.

"It's what he didn't say. He said nothing about you being safe. We need to get you out of here. At daybreak."

"At daybreak? Kieran, how do we plan on doing that? We've never gone out during the day. That's bad, right?" Andrew points out.

"We have no other choice." I point out towards the hallway. "They're all Vampires. Our best chance to escape is when they're sleeping."

"But our skin! We could get really hurt or die."

"What other choice do we have? Carissa's in danger. We need to get her somewhere safe."

Andrew takes my arm and leads me to the corner of the room. He moves in close to my face so we are eye to eye. Through clenched teeth he spouts, "Kieran, I know you think this is the right thing, but we're in legitimate danger here. Like I said earlier, we don't owe her anything. You should look at this as a win! You found your father. Look, we finally have people. Vamps. Like us. How many times have you looked outside that window and hoped for something different? Kieran, this is the something you've hoped for. *We've* hoped for. *Emily's* hoped for."

"What are you saying? Just risk someone's life because now we have hope? C'mon, Andrew. I thought we already talked about this. We have to be better."

"How about trying to reason with your dad? You don't know he's going to harm her."

"I can't take that risk," I bite back in frustration. "I'm going with or without you. But," I try to become less confrontational, "buddy, I'd sure like you there with me. We don't stand a chance without that million-dollar smile and smarts." A smile moves across his face. "Look, we decided a long time ago we value life regardless unless, you know, that life is trying to kill us. It's the right decision. You know it too."

Silence rests between us as Andrew locks eyes with me. Finally, he agrees, "Daybreak it is. So how are we going to do this?"

I smile, grab, and tear open both pillows and let the stuffing inside fall on the floor. "We're gonna need some protection." I take the cloth and put together a makeshift mask and cover most of my face and toss the other one to Andrew.

He looks at me and laughs, "You look like some kind of superhero origin story. You know, before they have their costume figured out?" Putting his own hood on, he asks, "How much time do we have?"

"Bout an hour. Carissa, you stay here. We have to make everything appear as normal as possible. We'll come back for you. Trust us. Andrew and I have some planning to do."

"You won't leave me?"

I walk up close to Carissa. For a moment, I'd forgotten how she gives me butterflies until I get close to her. "We won't leave you. But look, I want to be very clear with you."

"Yes?" she asks, fluttering her big, brown eyes at me.

"I've seen what you can do. You are capable. From here on out, we're going to need you to fight at our side. Can you do that? I'll find you a weapon."

She smiles a soft smile. "If you're willing to sacrifice for me, it's the least I can do." Without expecting it, she kisses me on the cheek, leaving me stuck in place.

"Hey, Romeo, let's go!" Andrew grabs me by the collar and pulls me. I follow him out the door, stealing one last glance towards Carissa and am met with a laughing smile.

As we go into our room, Andrew looks back. "Well, I guess I know why we're risking our lives." He makes his eyebrows bounce.

"Shut up," I laugh at him and push his shoulder. "So, how do you figure we get out of here? The same way we came in?"

"More or less," Andrew says, mischief creeping across his face. "First, remember all those cleaning supplies in the janitor's closet?"

"Ha ha! Yes, I'm already loving this idea," I whisper.

An hour later, I open the door and peek out of our room. Looking back at Andrew, I tell him, "Hang out here. I'm going to walk down the hallway. Make sure all is quiet. You stay here and work on our plan. You're much better with this part than I am." I shoot him a wink and slink out of the room.

The hallway is dark and damp, and the hum of the generator I noticed earlier is now silent. I hear the squeak of some rats scurrying in the corners and over my feet. Moving with my back against the wall, I know my assumption is correct. Everyone is sleeping, but I know we still have to remain as silent as church mice. Moving towards the end of the hallway nearing the break room, I hear the groans of the Feasters in the warehouse. My first thought is to release them into these hallways, but I don't want anyone, especially my father, to get hurt. And yet, I know I can use them to aid in our escape if things don't go as planned.

My thoughts shift to the night at the cul-de-sac. The night they trapped us. The night Emily was bit. The Feasters. Who was controlling them? How? What else does my father know?

As if on cue, my parents' song plays in the hallway. I follow the sound to my father's room and through the door, I could hear my father talking. No, not talking. Crying. Pleading. Putting my ear to the door, I listen. "I found him, Lilith. More like he found me. I didn't think this day would ever happen, but it did. I was sure every part of us vanished, but now..." My father voices between sniffles. "He's so grown and changing into an adult vampire. Can you believe he's been surviving all this time with Emily? Together. Well, they don't know where she is now. Despite that, I thought everything was lost." He cries, struggling to calm himself, "We have the girl, too. She's all that's left of the Croger family. We can finally finish what they started. But I'm not sure what to do with her or what's the right move here. You were always here to remind me of the right thing whenever I've lost my focus. I can use some of that Lilith knowledge. Help me know what to do." The flickering light under the door goes dark, and the room goes silent.

I put my back against the wall and mutter to myself, taking a page from my father. "Mom, tell me what the right move is here. You always said to trust my instincts. They're telling me we can't be here right now. We have to protect Carissa." Nodding my head, I decide saving Carissa is the right thing. I know my father will be furious, but I know I wouldn't be able to live with myself if something happened to her. Righting my shoulders, I put my hand on the door. "Sorry Dad," I whisper.

Chapter 18

Floor Wax

After Andrew and I grab a drink from the animals at the end of the hall, we head to Carissa's room. Andrew knocks, without making much sound and Carissa answers, "You ready?"

She's pulled her hair back and looks serious. "Let's do this," she whispers.

"You're going to need this." I hand her a broomstick which will work as a staff. "Make Emily proud." Instead of the normal tears which usually form in her eyes, her gaze is hard and determined.

"Okay, let's go."

We move like falling snow down the hallways until we get to the janitor's closet where the roof access is. Once inside and climbing the ladder, Andrew stops us. "Wait."

"Wait? We don't have time to wait," I say in a loud whisper.

"Just wait. This is my area of expertise," Andrew brags, grabbing two jugs of floor wax. He opens the door and orders, "You guys take those two jugs and get to the roof and wait for me." I recognize that devious look in his eyes and can't wait to see what he's up to.

When I open the hatch, I forget about the sun. It's a good thing it's morning and the fog from the night before lingers, but it will burn off in no time, so we'll have to move. I cover my head with the pillowcase, so it looks like a hoodie. Still, the sun radiates on my skin. Once on the roof, I walk to the edge to get my bearings, see what we're up against, and plan our escape. It looks like it's the same as before. Ten to fifteen Feasters move around inside the gates. It's smart to have them out here. There is just enough to send a message if anyone thinks they can check out the warehouse.

"Why are you doing this?" Carissa's voice catches me off guard, breaking me from planning. I find shade behind what looks like an air conditioning unit.

"Doing what?"

"Helping me? Why are you helping me? I mean, you just found your father and now you're leaving him. Believe me, I don't need any more guilt in my life."

I stare at her before walking over. "When all of this went down, when the Feasters took over, everything felt the way the apocalypse is supposed to feel. Scary. Empty. Hopeless. If it wasn't for having Emily to go through this with; to have each other during the darkest moments, I don't think either of us could have survived. And, then when Andrew came into our lives, I had a vision."

"Like a dream," she stares into my eyes.

I shake my head. "No, not a dream. More like thoughts of how I envision the world I want to see when we rebuild. Every Vampire and person are equally important because they are the building blocks to starting over. Carissa, you are important."

"But what my family has done to you. My mistakes. My stupid decisions," she chuckles, but not because it's funny.

"But we're beings just trying to survive in this world. Vampires. Humans. It doesn't matter. We make mistakes. Only stupid people don't learn from their mistakes."

Carissa's eyes get a little misty. "Then I must be the dumbest person alive."

"We all have our moments." We both laugh and Carissa's hands find my arms, and she moves closer. "What are you doing?"

Her eyes change from laughter to something else. Something I've seen in movies. "I'm doing what you've been afraid to do." She leans in and her lips touch mine. She pulls away, "Is this okay?"

"Um." My heart races and I feel my face become flushed as the blood races through my veins, causing my eyes to glow. "I guess so."

For a moment, Carissa's posture leans back. Then she smiles, "Oh, is this what happens when Vampires want to kiss a girl?" I snicker inside and lean in to kiss her back.

"Ew, what are you guys doing?" Andrew pokes his head out of the hatch, shielding his eyes from the sun.

I scrunch my nose at Andrew. "We were just planning our escape." Carissa laughs and spins around to face Andrew.

"Well, I hope it's a good plan because I heard someone walking down the hallway."

"Walking?" I ask, curious about the mischief Andrew was up to.

He smiles, but I know he wants to laugh. "More like slipping and sliding. It should be enough to buy us some time. But we gotta go. Like right now!" Just then I hear shouting from within the hatch. Andrew jumps up, throwing the hood over his head.

We scurry to the ladder and scramble down. "Now what?" I shout.

"Give me those." Andrew grabs the jugs of floor wax and starts for the side of the building.

"Where are you going?"

"Buying us more time. Just in case!" He runs off and pours the jugs of floor wax at the base of the garage door of the warehouse which houses the hundreds of Feasters. By now the Feasters in the yard have turned their attention toward the three of us. The zombies split up. A small group moves towards Andrew, and the others focus on Carissa and me.

"Alright. Are you ready?" My fangs drop and my eyes glow red.

"Ready as I'll ever be." She readies her staff the way Emily taught her and moves towards the first Feaster, a male in shredded hospital scrubs and covered in old, rust-colored blood. Its jaw, typical for a Feaster, hangs slack until it gets close. Then his mouth chomps at the air, the sound of teeth popping as they come together in anticipation of a meal. As it lunges towards her, she dodges left. With her staff, she upends him, and he lands on his face. With one movement, she thrusts the end of the staff into the back of his skull, puncturing the brain.

Meanwhile, the ping of Andrew's bat rings out. I look over and three Feasters lie still at his feet while one is walking around like a carousel, her jaw hanging like a door on one hinge. Andrew works his way over to us, "We gotta start moving toward the gate or we're gonna run out of time."

"Lead the way!" I tell him. My attention turns to Carissa. "Duck!" I yell. She listens and I slice my machete into the throat of a tall Feaster just behind her and with a swing of his bat, Andrew finishes the deal. The three of us work our way through the throng of Feasters. I'm impressed by Carissa's skills. Halfway to the gate, the garage door rolls up inches at a time. The shuffling feet of hundreds of Feasters press against the door as it lifts. Once it's up high enough, droves of zombies cross the threshold. The three of us stand frozen. "Kieran," growls Andrew, his eyes red like embers. "Remember when I said I was buying us time? Well, our *just in case* is about to happen." We watch as, one by one, the Feasters slip and slide like they are on ice, tumbling and falling on top of each other. The more each monster struggles to get to their feet, the more they slip and crash. Their moans grow louder with each fall. Andrew's plan of pouring the floor wax across the concrete is his most brilliant escape yet.

The three of us take a second to watch the show, like a slapstick comedy my parents enjoyed watching before the apocalypse. Just then, Milo opens the door next to the garage and yells at us. Floor wax covers his failing hairline and drenches his beard. He steps out from the door, shielding his eyes from the sun, and yells, "Come back here!" We dash to the hole in the gate, slicing and slashing our way through the Feasters in our way. I look over my shoulder in time to see Milo slip on the wax and end up hard on his back. He yells, "I'm gonna get you, you little punk!"

The three of us move through the hole in the fence and take off for the Camaro. Andrew holsters his bat and stops, looking back at the warehouse and whistles. He waits a moment before Starsky comes racing from around the fence line. He bounds into Andrew's arms, showering his face with kisses. "Andrew, let's go!" I yell.

We tumble into the Camaro, and I make it roar to life. We take a second to look at the warehouse. I see my father's gigantic frame fill the doorway. His exposed skin smokes from the sun's exposure as he walks through the yard of the warehouse hacking through Feasters. He doesn't break his glare at us as he walks towards the fence and rolls open the gates freeing the rest of the Feasters into the streets. I throw the car into drive and spin it around while fishtailing down the block.

Despite Andrew's cheers, I feel conflicted. My father is going to be furious, but in my heart, I know we have to try to preserve life despite our differences. Part of me understands all my father is feeling. Just watching how he would pay attention to my mother like she was the only person in the room when they talked, I knew back then if I could ever find love, I would love my wife the way my father loved my mother. But, if I've learned one thing in this mad, mad world, there's an obvious difference between love and obsession. Love is the feeling that you would sacrifice your own life to protect someone and make sure their every need is met. The way my parents cared for each other was love. Obsession is something else. Obsession disguises itself as love and drives a person to sacrifice themselves, and others who get in the way. Harold's obsession led him to willingly let what happened to his family and wife drive him to the edge of madness. That madness almost took our lives. My father? The look in his eyes matched what I saw in Harold's. My gut tells me he's obsessed with revenge and despite Carissa not having any family left, he intends on doing harm to her. I know I will have questions to answer, but this is the right decision.

Chapter 19

Boys Can Be So Dumb

While I race the Camaro down the streets, my mind races too. I bring the car to a screeching halt at the rear entrance of Sebastian Labs. "Hey, guys. Before we go in, we need to talk about something."

"Like the way you two did the smoochy face shuffle out there on the roof?" Andrew laughs. When he sees the seriousness plastered across my face, he pivots. "Sorry, I was just. I... I was just being stupid." I force a smile, but it's clear my mind is somewhere else. "Okay, man. What's up?"

"Look, I think we're gonna need a new place to live. Sebastian Labs isn't safe."

"You think they'll come for me?" Carissa wonders, fear consuming her words.

"Absolutely," I say. "But to be honest, I don't know how safe any of us are."

"Even with your dad?" Andrew wonders.

"I'm not sure. I don't think he would try to hurt me or you, but we don't stand for the same things. Down the road, it could mean trouble. But for Carissa? We need to get her to safety."

"So, what should we do?" Carissa asks, nerves pulling at her voice.

"Do you know a place where we can go?" Andrew asks her.

Carissa's eyes dart from side to side and her mouth twists like she tasted something sour. "I'm not sure. Here is the only place I can think of."

"Carissa, I'm sure your family has traveled. Any place would work even if it's temporary." I tell her.

Her eyes widen. "I know a place! My uncle had a cabin which we went to all the time on vacation. It's upstate, just a few hours from here. Avalanche Lake. We would go up there in the fall when the leaves were just changing, and it's quite secluded. I'm not sure whatever happened to it, but it's a place."

"Wait!" Andrew cries. "What about Emily?" He looks at me.

"I haven't forgotten. Of course, we aren't leaving without her," I reassure him. "Avalanche Lake. Okay. Is there still plenty of gas for the generators?"

"We haven't used much. I'm not sure how much is enough to get us there," Carissa says.

"Then it sounds like a plan," I say. "Okay, you guys have ten minutes to grab whatever you need. I'm not sure how far behind they are. Carissa, you grab the gas cans and bring them to our room. Andrew, make sure we have all the weapons and the duffel bag with any supplies we are going to need. Let's go."

The three of us and Starsky race inside and begin collecting the things we'll need to escape. Carissa heads to her room and is undoubtedly folding her clothes and packing them neatly into a suitcase. As I enter our room, Andrew is just throwing his stuff into his backpack and one of the duffel bags. When he notices Emily's things, he shows more care. He picks up her favorite sweatshirt, holds it to the faint light, and then brings it to his nose. He notices me and a rosy, red color fills his cheeks. "I miss her," he admits.

"She's not gone."

"I know, but…," his voice wavers as if he either doesn't know what to say or how to say it.

"Buddy, Emily's a wild horse who loves to run free. She'll come back to us when she's ready."

"What if she's not Emily any longer?"

"I've been thinking about this. Back at the house. She protected us. It may not be the Emily we're used to, but despite whatever Emily turned into on the outside, she's still the same Emily on the inside."

Andrew holds up the sweater and half smiles, "You think so?"

"Andrew, I know so. She's in there. When we leave here, we'll head back to the house and wait for her. There's no way we're leaving her behind, but we gotta get moving."

"Okay, I'm gonna pack Emily's things. She'll be so mad if we packed our stuff and just left hers here." He snorts out a short laugh.

I join in. "Ain't that the truth." I shove my stuff into my duffel bag and then head out into the hallway with my backpack.

"Where are you going?"

"Going to find some leverage," I tell Andrew.

"Leverage?" Instead of answering him, I continue down the hallway to Harold's office. Although I've checked it out before, my guess is that's where the cure is being stored. On the drive over, I thought about my father's obsession. Although it centers on what happened to my mother and the cure, I'm sure this is what The Circle is after. I don't know what they would use it for or even how to use it. It could be they just want to destroy it. That's what I would do... get rid of the threat against our kind.

I peek in, half expecting to see someone in there, but of course it's empty. Panning the room, I look for places they could hide it. I've already rummaged through the desk. Besides the compartment where I found the newspaper clippings, there wasn't more to it. Knowing Harold, his obsession would have driven him to keep it close like something sacred. After checking the back of the drawers of the file cabinets and finding nothing, I second guess my assumption and wonder if it's in another part of Sebastian Labs. I know I could just ask Carissa and get her to tell me, but I think it's important she doesn't know I have it. She'd panic and just give it away if pressured.

Frustrated, I start to leave. As I glance back at the painting of Harold and Franklin hanging on the wall, I pick up an award with Sebastian Labs etched into the crystal displayed on top of a wall mounted shelf and hurl it at the painting. It crashes with Harold's smug image, shattering the trophy into pieces. It's then I notice the painting's frame is hinged on one side and opens like a door. Behind the painting appears to be a secret compartment with its own metal door like those in spy movies I've seen. I find what I'm looking for when I turn the handle and open the small door. Like an explorer finding treasure, my eyes widen as I find a box with twenty vials of gray fluid which could be the cure. The box housing the vials has the word VAMPcura written in marker. I'm not sure if cura is an English word but put together it sure sounds like Vampire cure. My first thought is to smash every vial, so the cure vanishes forever. Instead, I take a breath and reason takes over. Grabbing the box out of the tray, I put it in my backpack and cover it with anything soft I can find and keep it close. I hurry back down to meet Andrew.

We head out into the hallway with our things and call for Carissa. "Carissa, it's time. We gotta get out of here."

She opens the door. "Okay, I'm here. I'm here." To my surprise, she's traveling light. A small suitcase. A backpack. Her staff and a buck knife I hadn't seen before strapped to her leg.

"So, do you know how to get to the house at Avalanche Lake?" I ask.

"Nope, but once we get to the highway, it's north. I'm sure we'll see signs for it once we're upstate."

"Well, alright," Andrew laughs. "We're winging it. I love adventure. Once we find Emily, we'll be on our way."

The three of us, Starsky, and the leftover pig Andrew has under some kind of trance make our way down the hallway. Our arms are full with our bags, supplies, and the containers of gas. Carissa, with the lightest of the loads and a free hand, leads the way. She's got a pep in her step and, like the rest of us, is eager to get away. "Thank you for this." Carissa looks back at us as she opens the door to the stairs. Suddenly, an enormous decaying hand grabs her arm. She lets out a shrill scream which sends Starsky into a fit of barks. Without delaying, I reach for my machete and hack the arm clean off with one swing, spraying blood across our faces. Anguished screams from the creature echo into the hallways.

Andrew pulls Carissa back and the two of them end up on the floor. When she looks down, the hand is still latched to her arm. "Get it off! Get it off!" Andrew yanks it from her arm and tosses it aside.

As they scramble to their feet, the door opens to the hall. Two large zombie-like creatures with eyes glowing red behind dead Feasters eyes enter. They look like the same ones at the cul-de-sac and the house when Emily tore through those Feasters. The two creatures move into the hallway. Maroon blood flows from the one with the missing arm and puddles onto the floor. Then, the echoing of heavy boots comes from the stairs and moves into the hallway. It's my father. His eyes are raging a bright red, and his snarl exposes long, sharp fangs. He stands behind the two, dwarfing them by a head.

The three of us scramble against the wall. Starsky's barking simmers to a growl as he curls himself around Andrew's leg. The hallway fills with uncertainty. My mind races for what to say and how to say it. Staring at my father's face, I try to recall a time when I'd seen him this angry and could remember only once. The day after my mother was laid to rest. He'd been so strong. Sure, he cried, but he remained a rock for me and for the family. But that day, he couldn't contain himself. Through the crack of the garage door, I heard my father screaming and throwing things. When I peeked in, he stormed around the garage, eyes glowing red. The rage in his eyes was something ripped from the pages of Vampire mythology.

"Kieran," he growls. "What are you doing?" I'm speechless. "Why would you risk everything for this girl?" He points an enormous finger tipped with a jagged, sharp nail towards Carissa.

I take a deep breath and think about what I need to say without making matters worse. "Risk everything? Dad, you're going to kill her. Your vengeance is making you blind. So blind, I think *you* are the one who's willing to give up everything."

"What do you mean?" He asks. The two creatures next to him growl, longing for flesh.

I soften my voice. "Dad, if you decide to go through with this, I won't look at you the same way ever again. This isn't who you are. You aren't a killer."

"Kieran, you aren't seeing the big picture."

"What big picture?" I step forward, cautiously pushing Carissa so she is the one further away from my father and these two creatures just in case things get out of hand.

My father transitions partially back to normal as he begins his explanation. "You already know the hatred the Croger family had for us. But it wasn't just them, son. The world hates Vampires."

"Not everyone," I point out.

"True, but believe me, son, our heads would be on the chopping block if things went bad. Sure, we've made some friends. Some human voices to help with our acceptance. But let's face it, no matter how far we get, humans won't fully accept us."

"But what about everything Mom worked for? It's because of her, we have the rights that we do... or did."

"That's exactly what I'm saying. The Circle recognizes things are different now. In their effort to get rid of Vampires, Sebastian Labs has done us a favor. Now is our time to rise and live in a world where we matter. Where we won't have to worry about judgement or ridicule. You remember how hard it was to attend school?"

"But at the sacrifice of what, Dad?"

He ignores my question. "Imagine a world where Vampires can roam free. Free from human oppression. When Sebastian Labs started the apocalypse, they opened the door for a chance for Vampires to rise up and live in a land we've only imagined."

"But we still have to deal with the dead!" I fire back.

"Yes, but now we can control them. Some of those experiments Sebastian Labs performed turned out to be some kind of hybrid creation blending zombie and Vampire." He steps between the two creatures and puts a hand on each shoulder. The two, with their red, dead eyes, respond by moving aside for him.

My eyes flash side to side, trying to make sense of what my father is telling me. Then I hear Carissa whisper, "Emily."

"Yes, Carissa," my father agrees. "What makes your father's creations so special is they can control the dead. Like alpha creatures, the rest of the zombies fall in line. And their size makes them formidable and quite invincible against humans. It's quite ironic, little girl, that in your family's efforts to get rid of Vampires, they have strengthened us. We've evolved." His hands flex, and his fingers tap on the sides of his jeans.

"So, if that's the case, what do you need with Carissa?"

"To see if she knows if there is any more of the cure. Obviously, there has to be, since you used it on Emily."

Andrew, silent until now, asks, "So, what do you plan to do with the cure? Destroy it?"

My father breaks into maniacal laughter, scaring me. "You think we would destroy something so valuable? The Circle is going to use it!"

"Dad, you aren't thinking clearly."

"This is the clearest my mind has felt since your mother died. As the leader of The Circle, the preservation of Vampires is the key to our survival."

"Okay, so even if the cure is here, it's not like you know how to use it."

"Well, I'm sure Carissa here knows how." Her eyes shift and her cheeks get flushed. "I will take that as a yes."

"Why would I do that for you?" Carissa stammers.

"Fair question," my father admits. "Because I will trade your services for your life. If you give us the cure and teach us how to use it, then we will let you live. We will give you the supplies you need to survive, and you can start a new life somewhere else." He flippantly motions, his hands pointing out of Sebastian Labs.

Carissa begins to speak, but I interrupt, "No. That's not a deal I'm willing to make."

"Stay out of this, Kieran!" my father growls.

"You can't just send her out there against those things by herself. She'll be as good as dead out there and you know it!" My anger boils over, and I feel the blood racing through my veins.

"It's the best I can offer!"

"First of all, the offer doesn't give any options. Death if she doesn't help you or death if she does."

"At least if she helps us, she'll have a chance."

I roll my eyes at the notion. This time, Carissa steps forward, "I'll do it. I'll do it. But I don't know if it will work. What happened with Emily was an accident. A fluke. We were just trying to prevent her from turning into a zombie. I don't know if it will work to make these things." She points to the two zombie-vampire creatures.

"Carissa, no!" Andrew and I shout.

Carissa spins around to us and reasons, "Kieran. Andrew. Your father said it himself, at least I will have a chance out there."

"Listen to me. You don't have to do this."

"Kieran," Carissa's eyes swell up with tears. "I have always loved your honor. It's what's drawn me to you." She hugs me and kisses me on the cheek.

"Oh? This is the reason you are so connected to her. I always thought about the day I'd see my little boy with a girl. It's ironic you're in love with a Croger." I shoot daggers towards my father.

Carissa takes my head in her hands and directs my face towards her. "Let me do this. After all my family has done to yours, I feel it would make up for everything."

"This is different. Way different," I plead, swinging my hands in front of me.

My father says, "You should listen to her. It's her only chance."

"If you make her do this, then... I'm going with her."

"Me too," Andrew agrees, squaring his shoulders.

Fury shines brightly in my father's eyes, causing me to squint. He growls, "Why would you make such a reckless decision!? You are choosing humans over us."

"Reckless? Look in the mirror, Dad!"

My father's shoulders heave. "You would sacrifice everything for this girl? Even as our family is now back together?"

"This girl is part of our family. Our new family that we've built over the past two years. Now that we've found each other, Dad, I'd hope we all can be together."

My father softens a bit, tapping his leg with his long fingers. "I want to be together. Kieran, I've spent the better part of two years thinking I would never find you."

"Me too, but not like this. Not at the sacrifice of a life."

Any softness there a minute ago evaporates as my father's frustration grows. He yells, "Given the choice between Vampire or this human, the answer is clear! Kieran, you may have grown up, but you have not *grown* up!" He steps back and opens the door leading to the stairwell and dozens of Feasters shamble into the hallway, their groans and snapping of teeth filling the space. The one-armed creature turns to face them and shouts a gravelly groan towards them. The Feasters growl back like they're actually responding. "Enough of this!" my father exclaims. "We will work through the details later. The cure. Now!"

My father's booming voice jolts the three of us to attention. I lock eyes with him, red hinting just behind them. If Emily were here, our chances to fight our way out of this are good, but knowing Carissa's skills aren't there yet, it's best to go along with this... for now. I know I have the cure hidden in my backpack, but I need to buy some time to figure out what we're going to do next. "Okay, Carissa. Show us where the cure is." Andrew looks at me like I've gone crazy. "What? I don't think we have much of a choice. So, Carissa, where is it?"

She looks up at me and furrows her eyebrows in confusion. I nod at her and shoot her a quick, knowing wink. "Okay, it's down at the end of the hallway."

I turn back to my father, "You heard her. We'll go with her to get it."

"He'll go with you, too." My father put his arm on the creature who still had both his arms, who responds with a grunt and a nod. He walks forward a few steps and waits for us to move.

Uncertain of what to do next, I narrow my eyes at my father before turning to follow Carissa down the hallway. At some point, I have to tell Carissa and Andrew I have the cure, but I'm not sure how I will confront my father with it. Protecting Carissa is the main goal. An escape. That's our best bet. Make it to the Camaro and go. We will have to take only what we have in our hands and the backpacks on our backs. The gas and extra supplies are still in the hallway. I lean to Carissa and whisper, "Hey, is there another way out of here?"

"There's a door which leads to some stairs like the ones we normally use, but my father chained them shut a long time ago to protect us. I don't know where the key is."

"Nothing else?" Andrew asks, now onto my thinking.

"There's an elevator shaft, but there's not enough juice in the generators to get them going." Then her eyes grow wide in excitement. She tries to contain it within her whisper. "There is a ladder inside the shaft. My father showed it to me just in case we ever needed it."

"Perfect," I say. So that's it. We will make a run for it, get into the Camaro, and drive back to the house to find Emily. Then, drive until we run out of gas and figure it out from there. A wave of sadness swells over me. My father. Despite what he's become, he's my family. We just found each other and now we have to run, not knowing if I will ever see him again.

Just then a crack, like the sound a baseball bat would make against a fastball, jolts me out of my thoughts. The three of us and my father's creature spin around in time to see the head of the creature with one arm splattered against the brick wall. Behind it, her red hair like fire blazing in the dim lighting, Emily stands towering over the

Feasters and even my father. Before he even reacts, Emily moves onto the surrounding Feasters, tearing through them with quickness, and with her hands, crushing skulls against skulls and walls.

The creature escorting us down the hall turns to charge toward Emily. With my machete, I swipe at him, severing his right leg at the knee. As it tips over and tumbles to the tile floor, Andrew jumps in the air and brings his aluminum bat down onto the back of his skull, crushing it like a watermelon, spilling out what's inside.

My father's eyes glow bright red and his mouth exposes angry fangs. Seeing the defeat of both hybrid creatures, he screams, "What have you done?!" Without control of the Feasters, they turn on him. He readies a knife and sets out to fight, but before he has a chance, he's overcome and pinned against the large window of the laboratory that houses the chickens. Seeing this, the four of us ready our weapons. I feel the blood flow through my veins and my body morphs into the full Vampire creature I became when we had to save Andrew. I feel my muscles lengthen and tighten as I grow. My fangs drop and my eyes blaze red. Although he's not quite able to transform fully, Andrew's eyes are a fiery red and his body appears thicker in his neck and arms through his long sleeve shirt.

By the time we reach my father, Emily has already cleared several Feasters by peeling them off and sending them into the opposite wall or up into the ceiling. Carissa and Andrew attack the herd approaching us. Carissa slides to her knees, tripping up two Feasters and then bringing up her sharpened staff through the neck of an approaching zombie and into its brain. Andrew brings his bat down onto the Feasters she's tripped. Starsky runs over the Feaster and launches off him and into the chest of another zombie, sending it back into two others behind it. Back to back, Carissa and Andrew pick off the Feasters closest to them.

I send my machete into the backs of heads of the two Feasters desperately trying to make a meal of my father's face. They drop to the floor, never to feast again. My father stumbles away from the glass into the middle of the hallway to catch his breath. We watch as the creature Emily has become annihilates the surrounding Feasters. Her weapon of choice has always been the bow and arrow, but she's so powerful, she needs nothing except her bare hands, which are covered in dark decaying Feaster blood, as is her face and the rest of her. Getting ready to take on more Feasters, Emily unleashes an ear-splitting scream. The remaining Feasters direct their attention towards her. My father stands frozen, astonished at what he's witnessing.

I charge towards Carissa and Andrew's side and help take out the Feasters around Emily. We defeat the few that are left and end up side by side facing each other, our bodies covered in Feaster muck. To Carissa's credit, she doesn't panic when the three of us tower over her. I turn to face my father, but during the battle, he'd made his escape.

When I turn back, I see Andrew approaching Emily with the caution of approaching a scared stray. Even hunched, she towers over us like a giant, breathing heavy. Although she doesn't look like the Emily we're used to, her clouded and red eyes peek with a green tint that gives her away. As Andrew approaches her, he whispers, "Emily?" She steps back. "It's okay," he nervously chuckles. "Well, this is certainly different." She covers her face with her enormous hands, her long fingernails still dripping with blood. "No, no," Andrew tries to reassure. "It's a good different." Emily slides her hands down halfway and then stops. Andrew flashes that smile which always makes her blush. Instead of blushing, Emily turns and bolts through the doorway leading to the stairs, leaving the door hanging by a hinge.

"Emily, wait!" Andrew yells, but it's too late. The last thing we hear is a distressed scream and the slamming of the metal door echoing in the stairwell. "What just happened?" he turns to us, concern and confusion in his eyes and voice.

We stand looking at each other and the carnage on the floor as Andrew and I morph back. "She saved us," I say, doing a mental evaluation, making sure we don't have any bites. We're good.

"I know that. Why did she run away?"

"You really don't get girls, do you?" Carissa jokes, a bit of sarcasm disguised in her voice. "Emily is the love of your life, but as a girl, she's worried about how you see her now. She doesn't look like the Emily we're used to anymore."

"So?" Andrew asks.

"Boys are so dumb. She's concerned you won't love her the same way you did before because she's not the same as before. Sure, it's Emily inside, but a girl is a girl."

"Ha! Emily's never worried about that before. She's always been, you know, Emily," I point out.

"Like I said, boys can be so dumb. That's her exterior. Rough and tumble Emily. Ready to kick butt if she needs to or at least sock you in the arm if you step out of line. Believe me, I know." Carissa rubs her arm, no doubt remembering the beating Emily gave her in training. "But on the inside, she's a typical teenager. She's a little insecure when it comes to matters of the heart."

"No, not Emily," Andrew declares, but uncertainty hides in his voice.

"Dumb. I watch her with you all the time. I'm a sucker for romance. You're pretty good at the things you say to her. Gets her laughing and blushing. But, when I watch her with you, I can see her brain working."

"I don't get it," Andrew admits.

"One day, I'm sure it will all click for you. Have you watched Emily pin her hair behind her ear when she's talking to you? Or, how about when she acts mad at you? She's really blushing and doesn't want you to see that, so she either turns her head or pushes you. To you, she's being Emily. But to her, when she pins her hair back, she wants you to see her. She wonders if she's pretty enough or when she turns from you, she can't stand how much she likes you, but loves it at the same time. She's a girl who's into a boy."

Andrew stares at Carissa, then to me and back to Carissa. "So, what's this gotta do with why she ran?"

"Dude!" I say to him, "Even I get it. She's worried about how you will see her now that she's changed. I mean, if what Carissa is saying is true, then she's worried she's turned into some kind of monster, and you won't want to be with her."

There's a long, processing silence. Then, as if a light bulb goes off in his head, he declares, "Oooh, I understand now. Gotcha. Well, it's too late now. She's gone."

"She'll be back, my friend. I just know it," I say. "In the meantime, what's our next move? I don't know what my father intends to do."

"Yeah, where did he go?" Andrew asks, spinning around to look for him even though he knows he isn't there.

"He took off right in the middle of the fight," I say, biting on each word. "He just left us to fend for ourselves." I'm upset that even though we saved my father from a certain end, he didn't stick around. Was he always this cowardly? Was he still plotting to get his revenge and use the cure? I'm guessing time will tell, but I'm convinced now we should expect anything. He put his own son in harm's way.

"I'm sure he had his reasons, Kieran. I don't think anyone is coming back for a while. Should we stick with the plan? Go to the house, find Emily, and head out to Avalanche Lake?"

"Can we wash this stuff off first and slip into a fresh set of clothes?" Carissa is trying to shake the drying blood and Feaster guts off her hands. "I don't know how you get used to this."

"That won't work. It's all over your face and hair too," I say to her, amused at the disgusted look on her face. "You did good. Didn't run and hide. You fought like a warrior. I'm sure Emily was proud."

Carissa half-smiles. "I won't kiss you with all that gunk on your face. Gross!" The three of us laugh and head to our rooms to get cleaned up.

Chapter 20

Having Faith

The moon is high as we drive over to our house, and I'm exhausted. Checking the rearview mirror, the smaller of the pigs we took with us rests her head on one of Carissa's legs. Starsky rests on the other. It's cramped back there, and I wonder how we're going to fit Emily, especially as the creature she's become. We've let the rest of the animals go in Centre Square where like everything else, they'll have to learn how to survive. It's a waste, but it would be cruel to leave them back in Sebastian Labs.

I glance over at Andrew in the passenger's seat. He looks exhausted. We both are, but I think it's more than the lack of sleep wearing him down. Emily. What's to become of her? Will she ever return to us? Can she become Emily again? These questions swirl around my mind, but Emily isn't the only one who's changed. My father has too. It's obvious he will stop at nothing to get to Carissa and the cure by any means necessary, even if it costs his own son's life. His madness has driven him to a point where he can't even see it. Or – and I shudder at this idea – perhaps it's been so long since we've been together, he doesn't even care. What's the phrase for that? Collateral damage or something?

But hope is something I still cling to, and I push off the idea that my father can't come to his senses. Before the world transformed into what it is today, he cared about everybody and everything. He didn't let the human prejudices towards Vampires affect his attitude. I'm sure it weighed on him like it did all of us but never to the point of vengeance. He even defended humans against the prejudice Vampires had against humans. I'm sure that was difficult, but with my mother's work as a Vampire activist, I've watched him work together with people and speak out against violence. So what broke him? Mother's death? Sebastian Lab's relentless pursuit to cure Vampires? Maybe the madness of the world today propelled him to this place.

Regardless of what it is, his plan is flawed and immoral. To use the cure to create Vampire creatures who can control the dead and use them as soldiers to eliminate humans so Vampires control the world is a terrible thought. Not all humans have prejudiced thoughts against us, so lumping them together would be a mistake. This isn't the time for this kind of attitude. The apocalypse is the perfect opportunity to start new. My mother always imagined a world where humans and Vampires actually worked together to make society a better place. I'm sure if she saw what my father was attempting, she wouldn't approve. Is it too late to change my dad or is it just better to take off and start over?

My thoughts shift as we pull up to the shell of the house we once lived in. The three of us, Starsky, and the pig get out of the car and look around for any signs of Emily. "So, what do we do?" Andrew asks.

I shrug my shoulders. "Beats me. Should we call for her?"

"Emily!" Andrew yells. "It's us. Your family. Look, we don't care what you've become or what you look like. I don't care. Just come back to us. Remember how we always talked about starting somewhere new? We're gonna do that. So, it's important you come with us, and we won't take no for an answer."

I look over at Carissa, and she's nodding at Andrew's attempt. She glances over at me and winks.

From the shadow of bushes lining the house across the street, we hear the rustling of leaves. Andrew spins around, a smile plastered across his face. "Emily?" What comes out of the bushes isn't her. Instead, a small herd of Feasters is all Andrew's summoned. Disappointment replaces his smile. "Well," he laughs, "I'm not dating any of these freaks." The three of us ready our weapons and work our way through them. When one of them gets too close to me, I hear Andrew whistle and Starsky lunges towards it, knocking it down from behind. Then Starsky latches onto the pant leg and starts pulling and thrashing like he's playing a game of tug-of-war with the Feaster's right leg. Carissa walks over and plants her staff into its head. I crouch down and call for Starsky. He showers me with wet kisses.

"I don't think it's safe to just hang out here waiting in the open. The garage is pretty much intact, let's wait there," I suggest, assuming Emily will see the car. There's a risk in having the car in front, but I'm doubting my father will recover in time and I'm hoping Emily will show up sooner rather than later.

Once inside, we pull out some things left over in the garage like some blankets and sleeping bags. Then we wait. Except for the occasional shuffling and groaning from the Feasters who must sense a meal is close, everything is quiet. I remember as a kid if my parents left me home because of a date night or a run for some dinner, I would get spooked every time the house settled or the wind rattled the windows. This feels eerily similar, except we hope the rattling is Emily walking through the garage door from inside the burned down house. "So, I've been thinking."

"Oh, this is gonna be good." Andrew laughs. Starsky rolls over like he understands Andrew's humor.

I smile. "Seriously. Carissa, has your father ever mentioned anything useful about the cure which could help us with Emily?"

Carissa sits up and her lips press together. "Remember, I told you, after those few experiments went bad, father didn't allow me to come to the laboratory as often. He spent so many hours trying to figure it out. Well, that and other things. He focused all his attention on bringing my mother and Case back to us. I know he always took notes, so perhaps there's something back at Sebastian Labs."

Uncertainty covers us. "Are you worried about Emily becoming normal again?" Andrew asks.

"Well, first, if Emily returns to us –"

"When," Carissa interjects. "*When* Emily returns to us."

I exhale and give her a tight-lipped, unsure smile. "*When Emily returns to us, we're going to need a bigger car than the Camaro.*" I chuckle to myself at my weirdness. It's funny what will race through the mind. For me, I am thinking about starting over at Avalanche Lake and how we are going to get there.

"There's always your father's van. I mean, I don't know what's inside, but it's big enough for all of us."

I cock my head, thinking about how it would be a good option, but also wondering if my father will come with us or if we will have to steal it. "There's a thought," I say.

We sit for a long time after the room grows quiet again. I know I'm exhausted, and looking at Andrew and Carissa's faces, exhaustion covers them too. It's not long before I nod off.

Sleep comes to me in an instant and so does a dream. I'm walking in the middle of the hallway where we've lived for the past several weeks at Sebastian Labs. The dull hum of the generator fills the air like a bathroom fan left on. There's another sound echoing through the hallway – the pounding of my heart. As I walk past the room where the chickens live, I peer in. Nothing's in there. When I look back down the hallway, I jump back a step. My mother's favorite chair rests in the middle, and she's sitting in it, smiling at me. The sense of dread I'm feeling eases as I run to her and sit on the floor with my legs crossed in front of me.

"Kier-Bear," she utters, her voice echoing in the hallway, surrounding me like a fog.

"Hi, Mom," I answer, my tone not matching my excitement of seeing her.

My mother cocks her head, and her eyes express concern. "What's the matter, Kier?"

I'm quietly collecting my thoughts, wondering where to begin. "I feel like I'm failing, Mom. Right now, things are far from better than when the Feasters took over."

"Leadership is hard, honey."

I chuckle, amused but respectful. "Leadership? This is not what leadership looks like. I don't know what I'm doing. Dad? Emily? It's a mess."

"Your father?"

It dawns on me that my mother doesn't know, and excitement takes over, "Yes! I found Dad! Can you believe it? After all this time, I found him."

"I told you he wasn't dead."

I look at her with frustrated amusement. "I realized that's what you were talking about after I found him. You kept saying it to me, but I didn't understand. I thought you meant cousin, Stevie, and I was like, I know already, because I was there when it happened. You couldn't have given me more information?" I snicker, throwing up my hands.

"If I made everything easy for you, you wouldn't learn how to lead. How is your father?"

"He still plays that song you two loved so much."

"*Unique is My Dove*. It was everything right in our relationship. It summed us up." She chuckles, and it swirls around me, ushering in pleasant memories of our time together.

"He's not good, Mom. He's... he's different. Not himself. He's obsessed with getting even and... and creating a society of Vampires and getting rid of humans. Not like him at all."

"You must forgive him, dear. He's lost and his heart still breaks for me. He always wished he could have done more to save me. As compassionate as he is, he isn't much of a leader. He's always let his emotions rule him. Being a leader was always my strength. Why do you think they made me leader of The Circle?"

"*You* were the leader?"

"Yes, Kier-Bear."

"I thought you were always into activism. A Vampire for change."

My mother's laugh soothes me. "Leadership. Activism. It's all the same. A good leader is an activist. A good leader is a voice for change. A good leader will get others to follow them. It's what I did. And, one day, Kieran, you will lead the same way."

"Me?"

"Why do you act so surprised? You've always been a leader. The Circle will need you."

"Mom, I can't even lead the ones I'm with. I mean, you should see what happened to Emily. I let her get bitten, and we tried the cure and it made her into this creature we can't control or fix."

My mother leans back in her chair and smiles. "Kieran, trust your instincts. You've already come across the solution right here." She waves her hands towards the hallway.

"Here? Is this why you brought me here?"

"Oh Kieran. I didn't bring you here. You have always controlled your dreams. They come to you to offer warnings or advice, but you always seek them out."

"Really? I've always feared them. Afraid I wouldn't be able to understand them like the night the Feasters took over."

"You cannot control fate, Kieran. Things happen for a reason or purpose. You aren't able to control it all, but you can control how you react. It's something I had to learn too."

My eyes search the hallway as if its shadows will bring understanding. "Do you mean you had dreams too?"

She smiles again. "I knew about my death. I'd seen it."

"Why didn't you do anything about it?"

"It wasn't my fate to control. Instead, I did what I could. Raise you right. Move forward with mending relationships with humans. And love you and your father."

Then, my mother looks over her shoulder. I look past the chair into the dark hallway and see glowing eyes at different heights. Feasters, like my other dreams, wait for my mother. "Oh, Kier-Bear. I have to go." She stands to leave.

"Mom. Why do you go with them?"

"As I've said before, they aren't dangerous. These are our family members, both close and distant relatives, who lost their lives in the apocalypse. I watch over them." She walks around the chair, placing both hands on the soft cushion. "Remember, the answers you are looking for are here."

"Where? How will I know?"

"You will know. Kieran, you will lead us. I have faith in you." She shoots me a wink. Before she leaves, she turns to me. "Kieran, remind your father that we discussed this many times. In order for The Circle to advance, it must include all species. Vampires and humans."

"What does that mean?" I shout.

"You'll know. Goodbye, Kieran. I love you," she smiles and leaves.

I inhale sharply as I awake from my dream. Momentarily forgetting where I am. I sit up, reaching for my machete, and look around.

"Bad dream, sleepyhead?" Whipping my head around, I see Carissa smiling at me from a lawn chair in the middle of the garage.

I can still hear my mother's last words from my dream like a fading whisper. *I have faith in you.* It's funny because the one thing I don't have is faith in myself. I'm not even sure about what we're doing. "Yeah, it's a thing I do," I respond to Carissa.

"What's a thing? Bad dreams?"

"We all have our abilities. Mine is the ability to dream badly," I snicker, rubbing the sleep from my eyes.

Carissa sneaks over to me so she doesn't wake Andrew. Starsky and the pig lift their heads for a moment but let them fall again. The pig nestles into Starsky's chest. Carissa settles on the sleeping bag spread over the cold concrete floor. "Wanna talk about it?"

I debate this for a second but give into Carissa's big, brown, pleading eyes. "Remember when you were training with Emily, and I told you we all have our strengths?"

"Oh, yes," she laughs. "And, you said your strength was that you were…"

"Good looking," we both say in unison, laughing quietly.

"How could I forget it?" Carissa smiles and places a hand on my arm. "I was like, 'Boy, he's cocky. I like that.'"

"Oh, really?" I laugh.

"It totally caught me off guard. Since then, I couldn't stop thinking about you."

"Is that right?"

She doesn't answer but bites her bottom lip, which I'm sure makes me blush. I'm thankful when she changes the subject. "So, besides being good looking, what is your strength?"

I smile. "Ever since I was a little kid, I've always had these dreams. Sometimes, they're meaningless. Sometimes they're warnings about things to come. And other times, they offer advice."

"Like they come true?"

"Sometimes. They don't always play out exactly as I dream them."

"What do you mean?" Carissa asks.

"Do you remember the first night we met and the three of us slept at your house and how we were a little freaked out the next morning?"

"Did you have a dream about us?!"

"Yes. Emily, Andrew, and I were at Centre Square. Some kind of festival. When we walked over to the swings, your family was there. You and Case were swinging, and your parents were pushing the two of you."

"That's funny because we loved Centre Square. Case enjoyed the swings."

"Well, you came towards us and focused on Andrew. Once you grabbed his hands, he was in a trance. Then, Case jumped off the swings and came toward us. With each step he turned into a Feaster. Before he could get any closer, your mother called him back. She saw what he'd become, but it didn't matter. She squatted down with her arms wide, waiting for her little boy. When he got close, he did what Feasters do. Understand, this was before we knew what he'd become or what happened to your mother. So, when I woke up that night, I knew something was wrong. I didn't know how, but I sensed Andrew was in trouble. The evening we left, we went in and checked on your mother. I had to confirm the truth of my dream. I knew by looking at her that it wasn't cancer."

Carissa sits back. I expect her to get upset, but she reacts with a half-smile. "That's extraordinary. It must have been hard. I mean it when I say how sorry I am about all that. I... I had to trust my father."

I take her hands and say, "I don't want you to apologize for any of what happened in the past again. We're beyond that, okay?"

She nods and gathers herself. "So, that's your strength, huh? I don't see how it could help you in a fight." She laughs, putting up her fists.

"My parents always called it a gift, but I've rarely seen the benefit. I mean, look at us. In my dream, my mother said I'm supposed to be some kind of leader. Great job, huh?" I look at my boots and chip away at some mud on the edge of the sole.

"Kieran, you are an outstanding leader. Like you said about your dreams, you can't always control what's happening, even if you already know something's wrong. You will figure this out. I have faith in you."

My body freezes as I look up at Carissa. "What did you just say?"

"You will figure this out?"

"No, the last part."

"I have faith in you."

A voice from somewhere else whispers in my ear. *I have faith in you.* "That's the last thing my mother said to me in my dream!"

"Really?" Carissa's eyes light up. "She's a smart lady. I do have faith in you. So does Andrew. Emily too." A soft smile spreads across her face. "What else did she say?"

Scouring my thoughts, I recount the dream. "She said, 'the answers you are looking for are here.'"

"Here?!" Carissa asks, pointing to the house.

"No, my dream didn't take place here. It was back at Sebastian Labs. She said the answer was back there, and I already came across it." My eyes race from side to side, trying to recall if I had. Harold or Franklin's office? The articles? The file? Yes! The file mentioned the cure. I dismissed it because it had all that sciency stuff in it.

Carissa notices a change in my attitude. "What?"

"Um, I'm not too sure about this, but I think I know how to help Emily!"

"You do?" Carissa's voice perks up, stirring Andrew, Starsky, and the pig.

"Yes, I checked out your father's office. Your uncle's too."

"You did?" Carissa's face changes to concern. "Did you have another dream?"

"Something like that. I found some files and some newspaper clippings. There was one file named V.A.M.P. It had all sorts of information about the cure, but I didn't pay too much attention to it because I was never great at science."

"I'm like, great with science," Carissa shouts, clapping her hands like a cheerleader.

"What are you guys talking about?" Andrew asks, sleep still in his voice.

We ignore him. "My mother said I had come across the solution. I can't think of anything else. That's got to be it! Carissa, if I show it to you, do you think you can figure it out? You already know how to give the cure." She looks discouraged for a second, no doubt thinking about the last time she attempted to help Emily. "Don't do that, Carissa. Give yourself more credit. What happened to Emily wasn't your fault. If anything, you at least stopped her from turning into a Feaster."

"But she turned into something else."

"But not a Feaster. Carissa, if you can read through those files and help find a solution, I think we can save Emily!" We stand up.

"Save Emily?" Andrew scurries to his feet. "What do you mean, save Emily?"

"I'm not sure, but I had another dream. I'll explain in the car," I say, excitement edging in my voice.

"Wait." Andrew asks, "Where are we going? We just got here."

"Back to Sebastian Labs." I move to gather our things and Andrew and Carissa follow my lead.

Chapter 21

You Will Lead Us!

About a block away from Sebastian Labs, I turn the lights of the Camaro off and creep along the street to Centre Square. Parking the car in the shadows, I turn the car off and look out the windows. "What are we looking for?" Andrew asks.

"Movement," I reply, glancing out of the tinted glass.

"Movement?" he asks.

"Yes, we need to make sure it's clear. I'm probably being too careful, but we have to make sure no one sees us go in. It's not like we can secure ourselves inside Sebastian Labs."

The car falls silent as the three of us and Starsky look for anything out of the ordinary. The thought of my father out there makes me very nervous and wondering if he's going to return with reinforcements frightens me. We have to get inside and look at that file. If my mother was right, then the answer must be there. Everything is quiet, which makes me apprehensive because Centre Square is never empty of Feasters. Tonight, there's not a single one. Starsky whines. "What's he sensing, Andrew?"

"We're not alone. He senses something. I'm not sure what it is, but usually he doesn't really have this reaction to Feasters."

"What should we do?" Carissa asks.

"Well, we won't know until we know," I advise. "Let's do what we do best. Blend into the shadows and see if we can get in."

"What if they're already in there?" she asks.

I shudder at the thought. "We're going to have to deal with that possibility when it happens," Andrew states. "The advantage we have is Kieran's dad wants you alive, so let's see where it leads us."

"It's not much of an advantage, but it's something," I agree. "So, let's get out and keep close to the buildings. Watch where you step. I'll lead. Andrew, you take the back. Carissa, you stay close and stay ready."

"I'm nervous."

"Us too," we say. Andrew chews on a fingernail.

"Let's just hope Emily is somewhere close by if we get in trouble."

We all nod our heads. She's already saved our butts a few times. My guess is she's close, but I'd feel a lot better if I knew for sure. The four of us exit the car but leave the pig in the back seat. What good is a pig going to be in a battle? I chuckle at the idea. Anything to lighten the mood.

We turn the corner and slink along the empty, abandoned storefronts. The clouds cover the sky, threatening rain. The smell of death grows worse with each passing day as bodies change to become more dead, either walking or laying. My eyes search ahead of us and towards the open field of Centre Square. The army helicopter still rests at its final place from the beginning of the outbreak. Around it, the sea of grass grows past our waists and the swings from the playground sway in the slight breeze, haunted, longing for days when children would play with them. The silence of the night rattles my nerves. I've never found comfort in the constant groans of the Feasters, but at least it meant things were normal.

We pass the third storefront and I signal for us to stop. Carissa's eyes bulge wide, like someone swimming with sharks. Andrew? He's cool as a cucumber. "Two more stores, past the intersection, and we're almost there," I whisper, knowing they both know how far we are, but I see Carissa's eyes settle ever so slightly.

Still no signs of Feasters or my father as we creep along the last store. We come up on the corner. I take one more look around and nothing has changed. Perhaps we are safe and steps ahead of my father. Then a thought hits me. What if a Feaster bit him in the skirmish inside Sebastian Labs and he turned? Perhaps he's not a threat any longer. My heart aches, but right now our priorities are to help Emily and keep Carissa safe.

I motion for Carissa and Andrew to cross the street. As we cross, headlights surprise us. My father's van starts up with a roar and the four of us are trapped like deer, frozen and unsure. "Why did you have to make this so difficult, Kieran?!" A voice, my father's, booms from a megaphone.

"Dad, you aren't thinking straight! This isn't the right thing to do! You've always told me to do what is right!" I shout over the engine.

"Talk is over!" He revs the van and creeps forward.

"Let's run for it!" Andrew yells. We dart across the street towards the entry of Sebastian Labs and Vampires cut us off, eyes raging red in the alley's darkness, fangs down, and claws at the end of their fingers extended. I feel my Vampire instincts shuffling through my body, but fear keeps them at bay.

Hearts pounding, we turn to run the other way along the sidewalk in front of Sebastian Labs. Through the shattered windows of the next storefront, four Vampires, ready for battle, jump to the sidewalk and hiss at us. As we cut across the street, the van has its sights set on us as we rush through the tall grass of Centre Square. The engine of the van roars like a lion chasing a gazelle through the Savanna.

From the shadows of the stores surrounding Centre Square, we can see red eyes creeping from every direction. We're trapped. We pass the large cedar tree towards the helicopter and scramble onto the top of it. After helping Carissa up, the three of us stare in horror over Centre Square as the red eyes of the Vampires surrounding us come into focus. Starsky barks in every direction. My father brings the van to a halt and steps out. He moves to the front of the van and stands between the headlights, "Kieran, there's nowhere to run. It's over. I never wanted this to happen! If you had just listened to me!"

"If I'd listened, Carissa would be dead."

"One life for the preservation of Vampires everywhere! That's a trade I'm willing to make!"

My blood races through my body, pulsing through my veins, and my eyes fire red. I look down at my forearms and see my muscles twitch and pulse as they grow thick. My fangs drop and my voice is unrecognizable when I say, "Do you know who you sound like?" I look down at Carissa. She nods at me. "Harold Croger. He said the same thing to Emily and me. If you go through with this, you will be no better than him or Sebastian Labs!"

The Vampires look to my father for his response. He steps forward. "As the leader of The Circle, my concern is advancing Vampires. There is no better time to do this than now. She's going to give us the cure and show us what she knows!"

"It's not there!" I yell. Carissa shoots me a confused look.

"What do you mean it's not there?" My father asks.

"It's right here!" I growl. Out of my backpack, I grab the box of VAMPcura and hold up a vial. "I've got it right here." I shatter it on the side of the helicopter frame.

"What are you doing?!" My father yells and steps forward. The Vampires hiss in astonishment.

"You will never get up here in time before I smash every vial! Step back!" I growl.

I glance over at Andrew and his lips tighten into a smile. "Leverage," he growls, his voice gruff.

Carissa looks surprised to see the cure in my hands, but now isn't the time to explain. I focus my attention on my father again.

"You wouldn't!" he shouts.

"Oh no?" I grab another vial and smash it. "Make your choice!"

My father looks uncertain about what to do next. He looks over at the Vampires and puts a hand up and they all step back. "Kieran, I am the leader of The Circle. It is my duty to advance our kind. Listen to me."

Like a whirlwind, my brain swirls with voices and thoughts. *You will lead us. You will lead us. You will lead us!* My mother's voice echoes all around me like a tornado, her words spinning around me from different directions. I reach into my pants pocket and feel for the leather square. Pulling it out, I turn it over in my hand, looking at the triangle and circle singed into the leather. The symbol of The Circle. I look at the other side and see my mother's writing. **You Will Lead Us!** It all makes sense now. I hear my mother's voice again. *I have faith in you.* Looking up at my father, I say, "Do you recognize this?" I hold up the leather swatch. "You handed this to me in a dream. You said mom gave it to you, and she wanted you to show this to me."

My father's jaw drops. "How... how did you get that? I meant to give it to you, but it was too hard for me because of your mother. I didn't give it to you because I knew how brokenhearted you were. How in the world?"

"The dream."

"How powerful your gifts have become, Kieran!" my dad points out, wonder and awe blanketing his voice. Confused murmurs echo from the Vampires surrounding us.

"You told me mom said I would know what it means when the time comes. I know now what it means." I stare at the leather swatch. Without warning, the wind sweeps through us, the clouds overhead part, and the full moon peeks through exposing a hazy ring. Feasters, attracted by the commotion, move toward us. The moon's light catches the triangle and circle branded into the leather, shining red and gold flecks. The wind whispers, *You will lead us*.

I hold the symbol of The Circle over my head, and the symbol glows in the moonlight. The red from my father's eyes shines less intensely. His posture softens. Rotating it from side to side, the illumination shines bright. The Vampires, so threatening a minute ago, follow my father's lead. "I know my purpose now," I announce, gruff still in my voice. "My mother, our former leader, came to me in dreams many times and I pulled this symbol from another dream of my father. I will lead The Circle. I will lead you!" Confidence swells through me as I shout the last part. The Vampires' murmurs swell as they seek answers from each other. Then they look at my father.

"Well, Dad, what's it going to be? You were there when Mom gave you this. This is what she had in mind, isn't it? Getting rid of Carissa is not the answer. Creating creatures to control the dead is not the right thing to do. And, most importantly, eliminating humans is not the solution. Mom was an activist who tried to work together with humans to unite us. She was a respected Vampire and helped to make change, even if Vampires had to compromise."

"But…" my father starts but words escape him.

"Mother told me to remind you that in order for The Circle to advance…" I wait for my father's response.

His eyes widen in realization. "…it must include all species. Vampires and humans," he whispers in awe.

My father steps forward, his eyes wet with tears, and returns to normal. Our eyes meet and the corners of my mouth curl up. I look up from him and look over at the Vampires. "Now is the time to start over and create a society where we can all work together for the greater good. No prejudices. No judgments. What do you say? Will you join me?"

Like uninvited guests, we can hear Feasters groaning and approaching. The Vampires look to my father for an answer. Feeling their stares, he looks back at them and then back to me.

Meanwhile, Andrew and Carissa have moved close to me. "Whoa," Andrew whispers. "That was some speech. So, is all this true?"

"Yup. I didn't put it all together until right now."

"Well, I hope they agree," he says, nervousness in his breath.

My father steps closer and looks up at us. "Do you think you can do this?"

"With your help and help from all of you, I will lead the future of The Circle. It's what my mother wanted. But I'm going to need all of you. Will you join me?"

My father's eyes beam with pride, and a smile settles across his face. Aside from looking a little older from years of survival, his face returns to the one I remember. He bends down on one knee and crosses his right arm across his chest. "I will follow you, my son."

Then, one by one, the rest of the Vampires do the same thing and a chorus of pledges come from them, "I will follow you." Thinking about what a commitment this is, I wonder if I am up for the challenge. I feel Carissa's hand fold into mine. She leans in to kiss me on the cheek.

Andrew's hand finds my shoulder. "I hope you're ready for this."

"We'll see. You got my back?"

"Always."

One by one, thousands of fireflies descend from the cedar trees and captivate all of us. Carissa looks up at the sky and laughs her flirty laugh I've grown attracted to. Several fireflies land on her outstretched hands. "This is incredible. I've never seen so many of them."

Then, in an instant, everything changes. Changes for us. Changes for Carissa. I step forward and put my right arm across my chest. "Thank you for trusting me. I know my mother did. We will rebuild society where everyone, human or Vampire, who is willing to help and to be part of something will join us so we can be of one voice and law for all." The Vampires step forward, nodding their heads in approval. "We came back here tonight because I think we have figured out how to use the cure to benefit all of us. It is with Carissa's help we might do this!" The Vampires look at each other. Confusion settles across their faces.

In one instant, a new dawn is shining upon us, and in the next instant I watch the astonished faces and hear the gasps of the Vampires in front of me. I look at Carissa and she has a pained look on her face. She looks down at her abdomen. In it, the sharpened half of her staff tears through her flesh. As we all stand in shock, Milo grabs my backpack and yells, "I've got it. I've got the cure!"

My father yells, "Nooo! Milo, you idiot!" Starsky clamps down on Milo's leg. He screams. Before he can respond, an arrow zips from somewhere and plants into Milo's neck. He drops the backpack and stands stunned for a moment before feeling the arrow and the blood seeping from his throat. Looking at the red on his hands, he peers over the Vampires. He sees their disappointed faces. Blood spills from his neck and in a panic, he leaps off the helicopter and stumbles before running off through the tall grass of Centre Square, redirecting the Feasters surrounding us. Within seconds, his screams fill the night air as Feasters corral him against one of the empty storefronts, tearing flesh from bone.

The helicopter shakes like something crashes into it. I spin around, expecting it to be overrun by Feasters. Instead, Emily's large frame towers over us, hunched like a fighter in a cage. Her bright red hair, matted with dirt and Feaster guts, drapes over her face. In one enormous hand, her fist clenches her bow and across her back lies a quiver of arrows. Fascinated, everyone stares, awe-struck. I forget about Carissa for a moment, who is on the ground bleeding and grabbing onto my leg. Emily pans from left to right at all the Vampires who have taken a step back. Their eyes have lost their Vampire rage. The helicopter shakes as she takes a step forward with her bare feet. She puts arms to her side and behind her while extending her chest forward. She takes a deep breath and lets out a scream, causing everyone to cover their ears and step further back. For Andrew and me, the sound pierces our ears, sending us to our knees.

Andrew gathers himself first. "Emily! Emily!" She stops mid-scream and looks down at him. "It's okay. Everything is okay. No need to fight. They're with us now." She holds her bow up and looks over her shoulder at where Milo's life ended. "Not him. He's definitely not with us. I think he's still mad about the wedgie I gave him." Emily's eyes squint at Andrew and she tilts her head, confused. "Yeah, it was hilarious. Talk about –"

"Andrew," I whisper. "Seriously?"

"Oh, yeah, sorry." He turns his attention back on Emily. "Sooo, a lot's changed for you, huh?" Then, as if Emily remembers what she's become, she covers her face. "Hey. Hey. Don't run away. You're still beautiful to me." Without fear, he walks right up to her and reaches up and places his hands onto Emily's, guiding them down. He smiles, looking at her intensely green-red eyes. "There she is!" Emily tries to move her hands back up. "No, no. It doesn't matter what you look like or whatever changes you go through. I told you before. It's always been you!"

I muster up the courage to get to my feet. "We've been searching for you." Emily takes both hands and gathers us up into her arms. I know she could have easily squashed us, but her hug is tender. It's Emily. She looks over at Carissa writhing in pain, the staff still impaled in her body, blood oozing out of the wound. Emily kneels down to her. Either Carissa is in too much pain to show fear or maybe she's just not scared at all. Emily puts her hand on Carissa's head and strokes her hair and groans, her eyes concerned. "Emily, there's still hope," I tell her. "My mother came to me and told me we've come across the cure in Sebastian Labs. I believe it's there and Carissa can help us. We can help you get back to normal." Emily steps back and nods her head. "We need to get inside Sebastian Labs. Can you clear the way for us?"

I look up and see the conflicted faces of the Vampires. Carissa's blood calls to them. Their instinct pleads with them to drink. I step in front of her and let my eyes pulse red. My father notices this and demands, "Stand down. No more blood will be spilled tonight."

Then he turns to me. "I'll carry Carissa and make sure she gets inside safely."

I look at my father and smile, "You sure, Dad?"

Emily taps me on the shoulder and grunts, "Dad?"

"Hey Stinky. It's Uncle Silas." Emily's eyes widen in disbelief. My dad had a name for all my cousins. Emily's name was Stinky because of all the trouble she got into, and my aunt called her a "real stinker." The name stuck.

"A lot has happened. Mind if I explain later?" Emily rolls her eyes and for the first time I recognize her.

Before my father picks up Carissa, she whispers into my ear, her voice weak. "I don't think I have much time. We must hurry, or I won't be able to help. Whatever you do, don't take the staff out of me. I will bleed out and I'll be no good to anyone. Let's hurry. Allow me to do one good thing to make up for all I've done."

I look into her pained, brown eyes, now bloodshot with pain and concern, and say, "Don't talk like that. We're going to save you, too." She smiles a half-smile as my father scoops her up, cradling her. I hear her groan in pain. As I hop off the helicopter and rush to my father's side, I tell him Carissa's warning to me. Having worked in a hospital, I know he knows this, but I feel better having said it.

Emily leaps into action and clears the path through the Feasters by shredding them with her bare hands. One by one, she crushes ten of them and waits by the corner of the building. We, along with all the

Vampires, rush to get Carissa inside so she can look over the files for the cure I'm sure waits for us in our sleeping quarters. I know it's in there. It's got to be in there.

Chapter 22

Don't Take Her Away From Me

"Bring her in here," I direct. With great care, my father carries Carissa into the room where we used to sleep and rests her on her side on one bed. Even though the staff still sticks through her, he props her up as comfortably as possible by wedging pillows under her. Blood covers her teeth, which has to mean she's getting worse. Andrew and Emily wait just inside the room while the others scatter throughout the hallways. "Here's that file, Carissa."

"Hand it over," she coughs. She opens it and drops all the papers which don't appear important. "I see nothing here," she mutters to herself. After dropping a few more pages, she looks at me and shakes her head. "I don't know what to tell you, I don't see it. I mean, we can try using the cure again and see what happens," she suggests. Then she calls Andrew, who comes over to her. He's not hiding the fear of her condition very well. Carissa notices it. "Listen, it is what it is. If we decide to do this, we are going to need needles and several IV bags. Do you remember all the supplies we used the first time? If there's not enough there go down the hallway in the room next to the generator. Go ahead." Andrew leaves the room, tears welling up in his eyes.

She coughs, and blood spills out of the side of her mouth. All of us notice but remain cool. My father runs to the bathroom and grabs towels and a bucket he fills with water. "Hang in there, Carissa." He dampens a towel and rests it on her forehead. She resists because she still wants to be useful. It's then she looks at one paper on the floor.

"There!" she points out, mustering up as much excitement as she can. I rush down, pick it up, and hand it to her. Her eyes brighten. "This is it, but I'm not sure we can do this." I sit next to her and look at the lined legal-sized paper. Handwritten on the top says, Hybrid Creature. "This is my father's handwriting. I know he knew about what he created because he sent me away to take care of my mother. Knowing him and how he fixated on everything, he tried to come up with some kind of formula to reverse what happened. See, these images show three subjects on the gurneys. This one in the middle is bigger than the rest. That must be the Hybrid Creature he was referring to." My father and I look over the paper and the drawings. I remember seeing this but thought nothing of it. Why would I?

Our focus moves to the other two subjects on the gurneys. Scribbled above one of them says, Subject: Vampire. And of course, two sharp teeth protrude out of the mouth with a red pen. I put those thoughts aside. My father reads, "Restorative protein in blood will stabilize HC while administering cure."

"HC?" I ask. "Harold Croger?"

"Hybrid Creature," Carissa wonders and glances at Emily. "Look at the other gurney." Above this gurney, it's labeled Subject:

Human. The three of us look at each other. Carissa continues to read, "Mixed with human blood and VAMPcura, the proteins will synthesize with the pure Vampire blood and reverse the zombie blood wholly."

We take a second to digest this. I don't understand it, but my father does. "I'm not sure if he could actually do this or this is just theory. It could be dangerous. Besides, we don't have human blood," he points out.

"Yes, we do," Carissa looks up at him like a puppy.

"No, you've… you've lost too much blood already. I don't want to sugarcoat it, but you're dying," my father points out.

"Then let my death mean something."

"Carissa, no. We can't. You'll die!" I yell, fresh tears forming in my eyes. "We don't trade lives. One life isn't more important than another!"

"Kieran, you're sweet. I told you that's what I liked about you. But you heard your father. I'm dying. Let me do something meaningful. Let me be able to make right all this place has done to you and your family."

We hear a frustrated exhale of air behind us, and I spin around to see Emily. In two big steps, she's at my side. She touches her own neck and then to her fangs. "Change," she grunts.

"You want to change her?" I ask her.

Emily rolls her eyes and punches me in the arm, knocking me to the ground not realizing her strength. Then, curves one side of her mouth like someone who's made a mistake. "You. Change. Idiot," she grumbles and points to Carissa.

Then it hits me. I look at Carissa's confused face. "There is one way to save you," I tell her. "I can change you. You can become one of us. You don't have to die."

Carissa falls quiet. Her eyes dart back and forth, mulling over her options, her face a mixture of wonder and fear. She looks up at Emily. "But…" Emily touches her leg and nods her head, letting her know it's going to be fine. "But you may have to stay like that." Emily shrugs her shoulders. Carissa looks at each of our faces. "No. I won't let you do it."

"But," I say.

"Let me finish." Carissa puts one finger up, stopping my words. "I won't let you change me unless we've tried to help Emily. Since I'm the only human here, and I know something about the procedure, we must try the cure first. We must!" Carissa coughs out the last words.

"Okay, but I feel we are running out of time. We gotta get started, like – now," I announce.

In one of the laboratories, we listen to Carissa, who looks worse now, giving orders to set up IV bags, needles, and the cure. The room is a flurry of activity. It's not long before we realize Emily is too large to lie on a gurney, so I rush and grab cushions from our sleeping room so she can at least be a little comfortable. Finally, we set up two gurneys which flank both sides of Emily. I look down at her and say, half-jokingly, "You sure you wanna do this? You look pretty fierce. No one would dare mess with you in a battle."

She smiles with her fangs protruding over her bottom teeth. "Not always fight."

Andrew laughs, "It's not like anyone would mess with her before either. The perfect combination of beauty and brawn."

Carissa consults her father's drawings and is satisfied. I watch with wonder as my father inserts an IV into my arm and then, even though he struggles to find a vein in Carissa's, his gentleness and patience find a way. He's also managed to stop her bleeding and make her comfortable, and he connects her to an IV bag to make sure she has necessary fluids for her weakened body. This is how I remembered my father and to watch him do what he loves, caring for people, brings a sense of pride. He won't have a problem looking for a vein in Emily's arm. Her arms are train tracks filled with pinky sized veins crossing over each other. I watch as he thumbs a dial, turns on a machine, and the blood from my body and Carissa's flows into Emily.

"Make sure my blood flows slowly... I have little left." Carissa tries to make light of the grave situation. But it's true.

Finally, my father sticks a syringe into the bottle of the cure and fills the barrel. Next, he inserts the point of the needle into a part hanging from the IV bag attached to Emily's arm and empties the cure into the bag. The gray cure swirls as it mixes with the saline. All we can do is wait.

This gives me a bit of time to process what's happened. They have accepted me as the leader of The Circle, and to be honest, I wish I knew what this means. I know my father will be there to guide me, but from now on, every decision is on me. That's a lot for anyone, especially a teenage kid who knows nothing of what to expect. There are going to be hard decisions we must make for the good of our kind. Vampire and human lives could be on the line. The first recommendation is we move out of here and check out Avalanche Lake as a place where we can live. Up in the mountains, isolation will protect us, and we'll have a countless supply of wild animals to sustain us.

Emily. I hope what we are attempting will bring her back to us, even though there's a part of this she must love. The feeling of invincibility must excite her. The ability to walk in the daylight without the fear of the sun scorching her skin must be freeing. But, deep down, she longs to be with us. With Andrew. Not looked upon in fear. At her very core, she's still just a kid like the rest of us.

My feelings for Carissa have taken me by surprise. I sensed a connection during her training with Emily. Since then, despite the naïve things she does, the thought of being together rests comfortably in my mind. She drives me crazy, and yet, I long to embrace her and have some companionship. The thought of changing her makes me nervous, even though it will be the best chance to save her. I know how to do it, but the idea of doing it scares me to death. Watching Emily change Andrew freaked me out. I wonder, however, if she even wants to turn into a Vampire. I know she's curious, but it will be a big change. It was for Andrew.

Speaking of Andrew, man, despite being a little fearful back at the warehouse, he's rock solid. He's the reason I'm able to focus and function. Having him as part of our family for this past year doesn't give our relationship justice. I feel he's always been there. A brother I never had. For him and Emily, I hope the cure works so they can reconnect.

We don't have to wait long before we can see the effects of the cure. Andrew, who's sitting on the floor near Emily's head, stroking her hair, interrupts my thoughts, "Kieran, something's happening." Emily's now asleep. Her breathing becomes more even. The veins in her arms relax and grow smaller, as does her neck, face, hands, and the rest of her body. This is quite different from the scary moments when we tried to save her after Case bit her. "I think it's working!"

All of us stare at wonder as her body transforms. "I think it is!" I feel my father's hands squeeze my shoulder. It's then I look over at Carissa. Her body is lifeless, propped up by the staff protruding out of her body. "Dad! What's wrong with Carissa?"

He rushes over to her and searches her neck for a pulse. Seconds feel like hours before he finds one. "She's dying, Kieran. This was too much for her. If you are going to change her, you better do it now!"

Fearing she's already lost too much blood, which is the case, I jump up and pull the needle out of Emily's arm which connects the tubing to my own, spraying blood on the floor. Racing over to Carissa, I pull the IV out of her arm and search for a vein. "Dad! Help her!" Realizing what I'm doing, he takes her other arm and slaps her forearm, begging for a vein to show. Finally finding one, he inserts the needle. My blood flows directly into Carissa's body. "God," I pray, "please let this be enough to save her. Don't take her away from me." I whisper, begging and pleading, my eyes tight and my hands holding her cold ones.

Every second feels like forever. I glance over to see Emily, who's asleep and remarkably looks almost as if she's returned to normal, but still, I'm not sure if this will be enough to change her back fully. What if Carissa's blood wasn't enough, or if Harold's theory was even correct? It's obvious he was onto something, but what about long term?

Shifting my attention back to Carissa, I notice her hand is warmer, but I can't tell if it's because I've been holding it or she's getting better. If giving her my blood this way works, there's no need for me to bite her. Deep down, that's my hope, shuddering at the idea. I shoot a look at my dad, encouraging him to check her heartbeat again. He does. Curling up the sides of his mouth, he confides, "Her pulse is stronger." Tears escape my eyes. "I think she's going to make it. What you did, Kieran, in that moment, saved her life. The decision you made to use your blood is the thing natural leaders are made of. I'm proud of you. Our future is in excellent hands."

I smile up at him and think how lucky I am. In this world that's so cruel to everyone, I'm able to have the people, both humans and Vampires, I care about most in my life. If there's one thing this apocalyptic world has taught me, it's the importance of cherishing what is in front of you.

"How do we know if it's working?" I ask.

"She'll sleep for a while. I bet Emily will too. It's best we hunker down here. I'll get some of ours to secure the entrance and do a sweep of the floors just in case those things got in."

Is he looking for my approval? This leadership thing is going to take some getting used to. It's something I'll need guidance in. "Yeah," I smile at him. "Good idea. We've got running water and some other supplies. We released our animals because we didn't intend on coming back. Do you think you can get some Vampires to see what's outside if there's not enough in here?"

"Sounds like a good idea."

"Dad, what are we going to do about *that*," I say, throwing a thumb towards the staff sticking out of Carissa.

"Not sure. It will all depend on if she changes completely. Either way, she should be able to heal, but we're obviously going to need to take it out when she's feeling a little better."

I think of how Andrew's leg never fully healed after we found and changed him. "But she's going to be healed, right?"

"I have faith in that," he whispers.

"There are times where faith is one of the few things that keep me going. That and hope."

He puts his hand on my head and ruffles my hair. "You've always been wise beyond your years. I lost both things. Faith and hope. Since losing your mother, I felt like I couldn't get out of my own way. She was always my voice of reason. During this time alone, even with the others, I tried so hard to imagine what your mother would think or what she would suggest doing. But the farther time separated us, the worse my focus became."

"Because she was always right?" I think about how many times she's reminded me. My father laughs.

"Because she always had a way of seeing the bigger picture. *Tsk*. God, she was so good at putting things into perspective."

We're quiet for a moment. Images of my mother play in my head and even though they sadden me, they're good and they carry me through. I completely get what my father is saying. "She misses you, you know. Well, at least, that's what I know from my dreams. That letter? She held on so tightly to it, savoring every word. She's worried about you." His eyes water. "She led me to you and brought us together. I just didn't realize it until you were right in front of me."

"That's your mother. Even in the next life, she's watching over us." We embrace, melting away any of our differences the past few days have presented. "I think we can take out the IV now. You're going to start feeling lightheaded if you give up any more blood." He grabs some gauze and takes the needle out of my arm, cleans it up, puts clean gauze to cover the needle hole, and then throws some tape over it. "I'm going to make sure we're secure and grab you some blankets. I'll get some for Andrew too. You stay here and keep vigil. When she wakes up, she may freak out.

I watch him walk out of the room and focus my attention on Carissa, Emily, and Andrew. "That was nice," Andrew admits.

I nod my head. "Yeah, it's weird to have him again. I'm sure he's got some things to sort out, but hey, all we have is time, right?" I say, then direct my attention to Emily. "How's she doing?"

"Well, I mean, I'm no doctor, but it looks like she's back to normal. Or, at least getting there," Andrew says.

"I hope there was enough of Carissa's blood. She lost tons of it, but her heartbeat is stronger, so I think she'll be okay. My dad says she'll be confused. Do you still remember your transformation?"

Nodding his head, he recalls, "Heck yeah, I do. It totally freaked me out. What'd you expect?" he laughs.

"Freaked out? More like terrified. Thought you were going to pee your pants." Emily groans a chuckle.

Andrew and I look at each other, grins plastered across our faces. "Well, well, well, look who decided to join our little party of the living?" Andrew cries, a teardrop falls, hitting Emily square on the forehead.

"Hey," she complains. "Quit raining on me, ya jerk."

I move over to Emily and the three of us embrace. "Oh man, it's good to hear your voice again," I say, relieved. "All that grunting and saying one word at a time stuff was weird. 'Me, Emily. Me crush you.' I thought, oh man, if this is how she's gonna talk for the rest of our lives, we're going to have to start using hieroglyphics like the cave dwellers did." Andrew snorts.

"You idiots couldn't say that before because I would have crushed both of you." I shoot a look at Andrew and we both agree with shoulder shrugs. There's no arguing the fact.

Just then, my father walks in, his arms full of blankets and pillows. "Hey there, Stinky. How are you feeling?"

"Uncle Silas!" Emily says excitedly even though her voice is still weak. "I'm doing okay. I can't believe it's you!

"If it wasn't for this guy right here, we wouldn't be having this conversation," he says, putting a hand on my shoulder. "I'm sure you three have a lot of catching up to do." He kisses her on her forehead and then leaves.

I focus my attention back on Emily. "So, what was it like being whatever that was?"

Emily takes a moment and sips some water we had waiting for her. "It was strange. Empowering. Unstoppable. Like, nothing could stand in my way. No Feaster. No Vampire. The more I fought to survive, the more I wanted to crush and destroy. It wasn't enough to just defeat anything." She flexes her hands as if she's imagining it. "But there was another side to it. I felt empty and... and lonely. Like I felt what it was like to be a Feaster. When I wasn't annihilating everything in my path, my mind went to this empty place like being so thirsty and drinking from a bottle even though there was nothing left. Hollow. Longing. Needing. So, I found if I made my mind busy, I fended off those feelings. So, I tracked you guys everywhere you went. Made sure you were safe."

"You definitely made sure of that," Andrew agrees, putting his hand into hers. "Bailed us out a few times."

"Then, there were the fireflies. For some reason, they wouldn't leave me alone," she chuckles, exhaustion still in her voice.

"You always loved them. Outside, I finally put it together. They were around whenever you were, so I knew you were close."

She smiles, "Stupid fireflies. Blowing my cover." We laugh. "Thank you for never giving up on me."

"We'd never." Andrew smiles and gives her a wink.

"Did you mean what you said out there? It didn't matter what I look like? That it's always been me?"

Andrew flashes a smile making her blush. "Haven't I always said that?" He leans down and softly kisses her lips.

"Seriously, why do you guys have to do that when I'm right here? Sheesh."

We all laugh. Our family feels whole again. It's felt like ages since we've been able to get us back.

"Is she gonna be alright?" Emily asks about Carissa.

"She is now. You know she was willing to give up her life to change yours. She almost did. But she's okay. She's one of us now."

Emily's eyes widen, revealing her green eyes, which now boast hints of red in them. "You little Romeo!" She teases.

My cheeks flush, and I roll my eyes acting like it was more out of necessity than want. "I had to do it. She was going to die. Besides, it was your idea."

Emily nods in approval. "We have a lot to catch up on, but right now, I'm exhausted. I need to sleep. Will you guys stay here with me?"

"Of course. We're tired too," I reassure her.

The three of us settle on the floor with the blankets my father brought in. I put a blanket over Carissa and do my best to make her comfortable. I cringe thinking about when we have to take the staff out of her. We probably need to saw off one end of it, so the entire half doesn't have to run through her. As a Vampire, her body should take care of the healing. This is more than a broken bone like Andrew's. There's going to be more to heal than that.

Resting my head on my jacket I've rolled into a ball, I close my eyes and sleep, knowing in the next few days decisions will come, healing will have to happen, and we will need to move forward with our lives. I wish a dream would come to me and reveal something, anything. I long to hear the calm voice of my mother and to let her know Dad and I are okay, and she was right about everything. My body is an engine running on fumes from all that's happened and needs sleep. So no dream comes, and I sleep until the next night.

Chapter 23

Feeling Different

The next night, a voice wakes me from my sleep. "Kieran. Kieran. Are you awake?"

I rub my eyes and see Carissa, still propped up by the staff, but looking well and what's more important, she's alive! I scurry to my feet and rush to her side. "Hey there. How are you doing?"

"Well, aside from the fact this thing is still inside of me like a kickstand on a bicycle, I guess I'm doing okay. I feel... different."

I take her hands into my own. "That's because you are."

Carissa gets a look of confusion on her face as she processes my words. "Did you change me?" she whispers in awe.

"I did exactly what you said to do. Look, you did it. You saved her." I point to Emily and Andrew curled up on the floor, sleeping.

"It worked? I had my doubts. And, what about changing me?"

"You were dying. You'd given most of what blood you had left to Emily and your pulse grew so weak." Carissa reaches up to her neck to feel for bite marks.

"You won't find any," my father's voice breaks in. "This guy here had the great idea to put his blood right into your veins. That way he changed you and replenished some blood you lost. Didn't even have to bite you. How are you feeling?"

"I was just telling Kieran I'm feeling different."

"Well, that's just the beginning. There are many more changes to come. I know this is the last thing you want to hear, but we're going to need to get that thing out of you. The Vampire blood running through your body is going to want to heal the tissue surrounding the staff. If the newly healed flesh bonds with the staff, we're going to have a whole new set of problems."

She squeezes my hand hard. "Is it going to hurt?"

"Depends," he chuckles. "Do you want me to lie to you or give it to you straight? You let me know when you're ready, but don't wait too long. I'll leave you kids alone."

"I'll be here with you, if that helps," I reassure her.

"It does." She feels her neck once more. "So not even a nibble?" We laugh.

I drop my fangs and smile at her, "Do you want me to change that?"

"No," she laughs, but this time the staff brings some discomfort. "We really need to get the staff out of me."

On the floor, Emily and Andrew are waking up. Emily looks as if she's back to normal, which is remarkable. Her hair still blazes red, and the red which mixed in with her green eyes the night before is still there. She's going to love how it looks because it adds a fierceness to her. Besides that, she looks normal until she stands. Then she towers over Andrew by a good five inches. "Ha, look at how much taller I am than you. All of you."

"Oh great! We'll never hear the end of this. Wait until you look in the mirror. I think you're going to like those changes too," I say.

Emily runs over to the mirror over the sink and squints, then with her fingers opens her eyelids wide. "Whoa. This is kinda cool. Don'tcha think?"

"Yup," I laugh. "No living with her now."

She comes over like she's going to punch me in the arm. Instead, she picks me up into her arms and we hug. "I'm so glad you're my cousin."

Just then, Starsky barks. He runs over to the three of us, shaking his body, deciding who to greet first.

Emily walks over to Carissa and looks her over. "Does it hurt?"

"Only when I laugh. Or breathe deeply. Or, you know, move."

"Well, you look like a warrior," Emily smiles, nodding her head in approval.

Carissa's eyes grow wide with pride. "I learned from the best."

"You're darn right you did."

"Emily, I just thought of something. Now that I'm one of you guys, we have so much in common. You can keep giving me fighting tips. I can give you fashion tips. We can totally stay up all night talking like best friends."

"Oh God, seriously?" Emily rolls her eyes and smirks. Andrew and I shoot each other glances and can't help laughing.

After the laughter dies down, Carissa asks, "Kieran, you can tell your father I'm ready to take this out." As I walk away, she grabs my arm. "I'm scared," she confides.

"There's nothing to worry about. I'm going to be right here." I try to reassure her.

"Me too," Andrew adds.

"I'm not going anywhere either," Emily smiles.

"That's part of being family." I squeeze her hand and head out to get my father.

Chapter 24

The Circle

Only time will tell what's in store for us. When the Feasters took over and it was just Emily and me, I held onto the hope we would find others and start over. After the first year, I felt hope fade because no one we ran into seemed interested in the future. Just survival. Having Andrew join our family restored my faith. Our small family proved we could survive whatever the apocalypse threw at us. Deep down, I've known just surviving wouldn't be enough. We would need to rebuild in a place where we feel safe, where we can provide for our needs, and build on the future.

The sun sets over Centre Square, painting the sky pink and orange like cotton candy. Emily shifts the Camaro into gear with Andrew by her side. I sit in the back as Carissa rests her head against my shoulder, still recovering from having the staff removed two days ago. She's adjusted well to becoming a Vampire, although getting her to feed on the pig was a bit of an ordeal. She'll get it. It's weird how someone who started off as our enemy is now part of our family. I'm thankful for her. I never thought about companionship until Emily and Andrew's own relationship developed. Watching them care for each other differently than just friends; I realized I was lonely. My feelings for Carissa caught me by surprise. I'm not sure what will develop, but I know now I can't picture life without her. She's smarter and braver than she gets credit for. To be honest, I don't even think she realized those strengths hid inside her, simmering under the surface, screaming to get out. It impressed everyone that she was willing to sacrifice herself to save Emily.

Speaking of Emily, she's back to normal. Mostly. The cure brought her back to us. Sure, physically, she's bigger and stronger than Andrew, me, or most anyone else in our new family, but she's still Emily. Fun. Sarcastic. My cousin. Inside, I had my doubts that Harold's cure could work, but after watching Carissa figure it out and it actually working, I know this is more than just a theory. Could there be others out there who were victims to Harold's experiments? Perhaps others we can add to our group? Or are there some failed experiments we should worry about?

Still, Emily hasn't completely returned to normal. She spent the evening after Carissa's surgery in Centre Square, testing if anything remained of the beast she'd become. Armed with two hunting knives, she walked straight towards a small herd of Feasters who'd gotten a scent of an animal. "You want some help?" Andrew asked.

"Do I look like I need help?" she snickered. With each step towards the herd, her body transformed not quite into the beast she was before, but into something pretty darn close. She grew in size, both in height and muscularity. Her eyes hazed over like that of a

Feaster, but behind it, they glowed red and green like beacons of rage. She hurled the hunting knives into the heads of the first two Feasters. *THWACK! THWACK!* Then, she finished the herd with her bare hands by smashing skulls and splintering bones. After, she turned to us and glinted a smile, exposing two sharp Vampire fangs.

"See, I was right. There's no living with her now," I whispered to Andrew.

"Ha ha. Like there ever was." He clapped me on the back, laughing, and walked towards Emily. "You know," he shouted. "I'm not afraid of you!"

Emily rolled her eyes and said, "You should be."

The two of them ran toward each other, pretending to battle. It's true, Andrew didn't stand a chance, especially in Emily's transformed state. After a few rounds of dropping him on his back, she let up a little and allowed her body to transform to normal. They frolicked for a few minutes in their play battle, ending up side by side in the tall grass under the full moon. I joined them and for a few minutes we didn't worry about the Feasters. We were just teenagers without a care in the world. These moments don't happen enough, so when they do, I cherish them by drinking them in and savoring everything.

Some big decisions about our small clan's future need to be made. Where to live? How to set it up when we've gotten there? As the new leader of The Circle, I met with some Vampires but also insisted on adding Emily and Andrew as well. It's a strange thing to have them look to me for leadership, often hanging on my every word. I look in their eyes for moments of uncertainty or distrust, but there's none. My father has been by my side helping me get used to this tremendous role; offering suggestions and helping navigate through the unique personalities of the Vampires I lead. When we felt comfortable with all decisions, my father told me, "It's time to address everyone. Let everyone know what the plan is and how we are going to do it."

"Dad, I don't know what to say."

"They respect you. So, don't be nervous. You are a natural leader. Mom thought so. Say, whatever comes to mind, it will be enough. Are you ready?" He leaned in for a welcomed hug.

"Nope, but let's do this."

"I will gather everyone."

Within minutes, I was in front of our clan, nerves racing through me. I tried to contain my hands from shaking. My father's nod urged me on. Something took over me. Call it a wave of confidence or perhaps an understanding of the moment, but I looked over the small throng of Vampires, thirty in all. My mother's voice offered reassurance from some far-off place. *You will lead us.* I looked over the group staring each Vampire in the eye like a coach ready to prepare a team for a big game. But this wasn't a game. Our lives are at stake and what we do and how we do it is the difference between life and death, between success and failure.

Steadying my hands and nerves I spoke, never once letting my voice waver, "Most of us here can remember a time when Vampires faced discrimination and experienced life as secondhand citizens in a world where, with few exceptions, people never accepted us or cared to learn more about us. So, laws were created to keep us in line to prove we were worthy enough to exist alongside humans." The Vampires nodded their heads in agreement. "But what many of us do not remember, because so many of our elders are now dead, is that there was a time when Vampires also didn't treat humans very well. We've heard stories of hunts and unwanted turnings of humans. A time when, as my grandfather himself once said, we were things folklore came from. So, there is plenty of blame to go around between us and them. But I know all of us can relate with a human we considered a friend or a co-worker who extended respect, not out of fear but of genuine understanding that no one is better than the other.

"We now have an opportunity to restart things. To change how they were in the past when we were driven by vengeance," I glanced at my father who tightened his lips and nodded his head. "From this day on, we will commit to doing my mother's work. We will give opportunity to any human or Vampire willing to join us. But as equals. We are going to need each other if we plan on starting over, not just to survive but to thrive. If a human decides they can't get past our differences, we will give them the supplies they need and send them on their way. If anyone foolishly takes action against us, then The Circle will decide what to do with one voice and we will act. This is the way it has to be if we plan on living in this world that just wants to eat us."

To my surprise, every Vampire dropped to one knee and put their right arms across their chests in agreement. Then they stood up.

"The Circle has decided our best chance at survival is elsewhere. This city is run through and there aren't many resources left to nourish ourselves. Several hours from here is Avalanche Lake. It's set up in the mountains. Carissa's family used to have a home there, and she remembers always seeing animals like elk and deer whenever she would visit. The lake will supply enough water for us and anyone else who wants to join us. It's a large enough place for us to stay. From there we will move from house to house; if they are empty, we'll set up our own places. It is there we will accept each other and anyone else willing to join us, serve each other how my mother always wanted, and protect each other because, after all, we are Vampires!" This time they cheered, slammed their arms across their chests, and let their eyes glow red.

I looked over and saw Emily and Andrew beaming and nodding their heads. Carissa? Her mouth opened in awe. From behind me, my father put both hands on my shoulder and squeezed in approval.

So, we are off to Avalanche Lake to start over. Out of the window, Feasters stare at our caravan as we drive by and change direction to follow. I look over my shoulder to see the two vans full of Vampires follow behind us. The truth is, we don't know what to expect when we get there, but The Circle agreed this would be the best place to start over. I'm optimistic that in the land of Feasters we are stronger because of our numbers and our dedication to each other and will to survive. My hope is restored.

Acknowledgments

Words cannot express the level of gratitude for the team of people who have been part of this journey. If it wasn't for these people, this novel wouldn't be nearly as polished.

First, I would like to thank my beautiful wife, Veronica, for your patience above all while I pursue my dream. Without your support, I simply couldn't do this. Thank you for the endless reads and allowing me to talk through my ideas despite the time of day.

Thank you, Avery Poznanski. As I've stated before, you're brilliant. We've worked together for three books now and each time, you continue to dazzle with your knowledge of the written word. UCLA is lucky to have you!

To Angelica, Carissa, Scott, my nephew, and Scott, my buddy, and Ava, thank you for taking the time to read through Feasters: The Circle. Your input and edits were truly valuable for me.

I want to give a huge shout out to fellow author and friend, Jerry Roth. I feel like we've been on this journey together. Your knowledge about writing is priceless. Most of all, I appreciate our chats and your camaraderie. Our time is coming, my friend.

I'm not sure if he will ever see this but thank you to Matisyahu for writing such an inspirational song, *Unique is My Dove*. When I heard it, it instantly became the love song to my wife and its message is a constant thread throughout this book.

The most important thank you goes to my readers who have picked up my books and enjoyed them. I am honored and humbled. You are truly the motivation behind why I keep writing.

About the Author

Born in New York City and raised on Long Island, Solomon Petchers has always had an affinity for scary stories where friends come together to defeat whatever bad guy or entity they face. It's no wonder that Stephen King is his favorite author. After getting his teaching degree, he moved to Southern California, where he spent all of his 25 years in education. Currently, Solomon lives in Murrieta, California with his wife, Veronica, and three amazing children. When he's not writing or teaching, Solomon spends time with family or going on dates with his wife. His favorite choice of movie? Anything suspenseful or outright scary! In 2019, he fulfilled a lifelong dream and released his debut novel, A Ghost in the Attic. In 2020, he unleashed Feasters: An Apocalyptic Tale. This award-winning novel blended vampire and zombie genres in an exciting, believable way.

Follow Solomon Petchers

Website: www.solomonpetchers.com

Facebook: @authorsolomonpetchers

Twitter: @solomonpetchers

Instagram: solomon_petchers

If You Loved Feasters, Try Solomon Petchers' Debut Novel

When 5th grader Samson O'Keefe is forced to move from his home in Ohio, he quickly learns that *strange things* happen in his new home. It is what's living, or not really living at all, in the attic that separates this house from other houses he's lived in. Samson has to rely on his new friends, Moose, who has a secret of his own, and Nathaniel, a third grade brainiac, to help break Mr. Henderson's spell. Fail and he may get *swept away* just like his mother and the other three families that lived there before him.

"This story has the quirkiness of an R.L. Stine Goosebumps novel, but a heartfelt storyline and endearing friendship like a Stephen King novel."

-- M. L. Crane

Call To Action

FOR READERS:

You can sign up for Solomon Petchers' newsletter, with giveaways and blog information, at www.solomonpetchers.com

<u>A REQUEST FROM THE AUTHOR:</u>

If you loved this book and have a moment to spare, I would really appreciate a short review on the site where you bought this book. Your help in spreading the word is more appreciated than I can say, and the reviews make an enormous difference in helping new readers find my books. This is true for all authors.

- Solomon

NOVELS BY SOLOMON PETCHERS

A GHOST IN THE ATTIC
FEASTERS: AN APOCALYPTIC TALE
FEASTERS: THE CIRCLE

www.ingramcontent.com/pod-product-compliance
Lightning Source LLC
Chambersburg PA
CBHW061613190726
48288CB00007B/2295